Remembering Rose
Mapleby Memories Book 1

By Sheila Claydon

Books We Love
A quality publisher of genre fiction.
Airdrie Alberta

Digital ISBN 978-1-77299-133-8
Print ISBN 978-1-77299-134-5

2nd edition
Copyright 2016 by Sheila Claydon
Cover art by Michelle Lee Copyright 2016

Dedication

To Rose, whose picture started it all.

Chapter One

I wasn't expecting the world to turn into such a scary place the moment Leah was born. While I was pregnant I didn't think much beyond how I was going to love taking her for a walk in her stroller, mainly because it was the only new thing she was going to have. Everything else was coming from the Pavalak family collection.

Before I became Mrs. Daniel Ryan my name was Rachel Pavalak, and everyone around here knows the Pavalak girls. There are seven of us, all with children. I'm the youngest, the last to produce, so when Leah arrived she already had fifteen cousins, and my parents had so much outgrown baby stuff in their barn they were threatening to hold a garage sale. Instead they brought most of it over to our cottage and drove away before we had time to unpack the boxes, so buying new things for her would not only have been a waste of money, it would have caused a riot. I did insist on a new stroller though: a red one.

"I just want her to have one thing of her own," I said when Daniel objected to the price tag.

"Rachel, your parents have at least three strollers in their barn, all of them in working order, so what's the sense of spending this sort of money on something we can have for free?"

As I couldn't think of a valid reason I resorted to the pregnant woman's ultimate weapon. Tears. So by the time Leah was born, the red stroller was waiting for her along with freshly washed piles of second-hand clothes, a crib that had been used by at least four of her cousins, and all the other free stuff I still needed to sort through.

Not that it was entirely free. The payback was that I had to listen to the Pavalak family advice, all of it, which is how I learned that the world is a scary place. Until I had Leah I was the happy-go-lucky Pavalak sister. Now I was the depressed one. I know all about crib death, choking on small objects, croup, asthma, eczema, bacterial meningitis, drowning in a bath and the most important thing of all, not letting my baby near a single nut until she is at least five years old, so when I went into the nursery early one morning in May I should have been ready for anything. I wasn't though, and when I saw a complete stranger bending over Leah's crib I did what any other new mother would do. I screamed.

Daniel arrived dripping from the shower. He was still trying to fix a towel around his middle when he burst into the room. "What's the matter? Has something happened to Leah?"

I had even managed to infect him with my irrational fears and that was a real achievement I can tell you, because before Leah, Daniel never worried about anything.

I didn't take my eyes off the woman as I edged towards the crib. "What is she doing here?"

I took two steps forward as I spoke, grabbed her shoulder and spun her around. Daniel's voice had an edge to it. "Who? What are you talking about, Rachel?"

I tightened my grip, or at least that is what I intended to do, but somehow she wriggled free and made for the door. With a cry of alarm, I shouted to Daniel to stop her. He stared at me as if I were mad and then very carefully lifted Leah from the crib and carried her through to the living room. I heard him pick up the phone at the very moment the woman put her finger to her lips, gave me a sort of 'see you later' nod, and disappeared.

I was staring at the space she had left behind her when Daniel returned. He was still carrying Leah who was awake now and rooting around for my breast. I reached for her, feeling the overwhelming love I always feel when it's time to feed her, but Daniel didn't give her to me like he usually did. Instead he lied. "Your mother just called. She's coming for breakfast. She said something about pancakes."

Daniel is such a bad liar that at any other time I would have laughed but I was too freaked out to call him on this one. Besides, even without the pancakes, I was glad my mother was coming.

* * *

By the time she arrived Daniel had given in and Leah was halfway through her early morning feed. He hadn't left my side though, not for a minute, not even to get dressed. He was still wrapped in a towel and his hair had dried in a tangle, a sure sign he was worried. Normally he gels and spikes his hair before he even goes searching for his underwear.

Ma came in like she always does, full of breezy, no nonsense practicality, and sat on the bed next to me. When Leah, drowsy-drunk from a surfeit of milk, finally slipped off my nipple, she took her from me and began to rub her back. With an audible sigh of relief my husband left us to it.

"Daniel says you've been hallucinating again." She has never been one to mince words, my mother. "He's going to ask Doctor Gove to call in to see you when he's finished morning surgery."

"I wasn't seeing things, Ma. She was standing beside Leah's cot. I touched her for goodness sake. I put my hand on her shoulder and touched her."

I didn't mean to raise my voice but somehow it came out as a shout that was loud enough to bring Daniel running again. He halted in the doorway and I saw him and my mother exchange worried glances. I knew what that meant. They thought my brief bout of post-natal depression was back and with it all the paranoid thoughts I'd had in the first few weeks after Leah was born. Great! As that meant they weren't going to believe a single word I said, I decided there was no point in making things more difficult for myself. Besides, I'm a better liar than Daniel.

"I guess I must have been half asleep," I ducked my head and fussed with the front of my pajamas so they couldn't see how confused I was. The woman had been there. I had felt my fingers bite into her shoulder, heard her gasp as I spun her around, and yet Daniel hadn't seen a thing. And

7

the way she left was odd too. That little half wave as if she already knew me, as if we were halfway to being friends. I wasn't going to work it out if Doctor Gove started prescribing again though. I'd only just come off medication so unless I could outsmart him, Daniel and Ma, I would be back on antidepressants by the end of the day.

I heard the relief in my mother's voice as she accepted my excuse, stood up and walked across to the door. "You're just tired from all those night feeds Rachel, so how about going back to bed for an hour or two while I look after Leah."

Anyone who doesn't know my mother like I do wouldn't have realized she was humoring me. They would have thought she was just looking for an excuse to cuddle her latest granddaughter. Her maternal instinct, always shaky, had finally bitten the dust around the time her sixth grandchild was born however. Nowadays she only turned out when there was a crisis, so the fact that she was here at all was scary. It was still better than being on my own with Daniel though, and trying to pretend that everything was fine between us when we both knew it wasn't.

* * *

I lay on the bed with my eyes closed for a full ten minutes until I heard Daniel start up the car. Good. That meant he had finally gone to open up the shop, leaving Ma to look after me until Doctor Gove arrived. I knew she would be watching morning TV while Leah slept on the couch beside her because she and Daniel would have agreed it wasn't safe to leave her unsupervised. With a sigh that was a mixture of frustration and relief, I swung my legs over the side of the bed and tiptoed across the floor.

The door to the nursery was slightly ajar and I pushed it open. The room, with its frieze of colorful animals marching across the white paintwork, was the same as always. There was a pile of diapers stacked beneath the changing table, Leah's blankets were thrown across the nursing chair I never used, and the musical mobile Daniel had fixed over her cot was still playing softly. As I leaned forward to turn it off I frowned. Who had turned it on? Daniel? Ma? And if they had, then why, because they obviously didn't intend to put Leah back into the nursery until Doctor Gove gave them the all clear.

For the briefest moment I wondered if they were right after all. Perhaps I had been imagining things and in my confusion had turned on Leah's mobile myself, except I knew I hadn't. I never switched it on until she was wide awake and smiling. Then we watched it while I sang to her. It was a routine we both loved, me because of her toothless grin, and Leah because she loved the attention.

I stood beside the cot trying to calm my thoughts. If I hadn't turned it on, and Ma and Daniel hadn't, well that only left one other person. Had the woman turned it on while she was standing watching Leah and I just hadn't noticed, or had she come back?

* * *

Dr. Gove arrived at midday. By then Ma had spooned some pureed carrot into Leah's eager mouth while I had a shower and got dressed. Then she had handed her over to me for her lunchtime feed. All the time I was nursing her Ma stayed with me and chatted about nothing in particular while we both pretended it wasn't because she didn't trust me to be on my own with Leah.

To be fair to her and Daniel they both had reason to be worried. I was so depressed after Leah was born that I spent all my time in pajamas and only brushed my hair and cleaned my teeth when they told me to. It was hard on the whole family but everyone had helped, especially Ma, bringing casseroles and cakes and taking away piles of dirty washing. I'll always be grateful. None of them had the first clue what was the matter though, and I couldn't explain.

I heard them talking while they sprayed the kitchen counter with disinfectant and scrubbed my kitchen floor. *The problem with Rachel is that Ma spoiled her. She was such a cute baby that she gave in to all her temper tantrums.* That was my oldest sister, Hester.

I knew she'd be like this. As soon as I heard she was pregnant I said so, didn't I Ma? I said she wouldn't cope with the sleepless nights and all the washing and cleaning, not Rachel, because she never had to help around the house like we did when we were kids. That was Ruth. She always had too much to say even when she was being kind, which wasn't often.

There were other remarks too, some so hurtful that I've locked them away at the back of my mind so I don't have to remember them. That's the problem with the Pavalak family; everyone has an opinion. And they especially have an opinion about me because I was born long after the younger ones had started school, at about the time when the oldest ones were thinking of leaving home, so they all think they know better than me.

It was Daniel's Mum who realized I was ill. She lives thousands of miles away because she met a big, burly Australian after Daniel's Dad died, and he swept her off her feet and far away across the Pacific Ocean. The distance and the expense mean she doesn't visit often and Leah was almost a month old before she saw her. By then I was having several panic attacks a week and had begun to believe that everyone was against me. I was so sure they were making plans to take Leah away that I refused to leave her alone, even for a second. I even dragged her crib out of the nursery and jammed it into the cramped space beside the bed. Then I hung a toy with jingly bells on the door handle so I would wake up if someone tried to take her in the middle of the night. I hardly slept, and when I did I had such vivid dreams that it was worse than being awake.

Daniel's Mum took one look at me, and at the mess the house was in despite Ma's best efforts, and marched me off to the local surgery. Although Dr. Gove is old and pretends to be crotchety, he's a good doctor. It didn't take him more than a few minutes to diagnose post natal depression. He prescribed a low dose of anti-depressants and told me to ignore the housework, sleep when Leah was sleeping, and take her for a brisk walk as often as I could. All really simple stuff, and in less than a month the grey fog I'd been living in lifted and I began to smile again. I stopped imagining things too, stopped thinking people wanted to harm my baby.

I know I'm one of the lucky ones and I'm grateful, truly I am. I could have taken a lot longer to recover. I could have become addicted to the anti-depressants or become so anxious that it began to affect Leah. I've heard of women who are still depressed when their children start school and the thought of being like that makes my heart ache for them. Being depressed even briefly has its downside though and Dr. Gove warned me about it when I was well enough to listen.

"It will be a while before people forget Rachel. Each time you have a bad day, and you will have them, everyone is going to worry that it's all starting up again, especially your husband."

A wise man, Dr. Gove, and he was right. Even after I was off the meds and back to being a fully functioning mum, I was aware of the raised eyebrows and the muttered remarks. Recovering from a broken leg would have been easier because then all my sisters and Ma and Pa would understand and sympathize, but they never accepted my depression. It's for other people you see, the ones who can't cope, the ones my judgmental family dismiss as losers.

Daniel's not judgmental but my behavior changed him too. He wouldn't talk about it though; not to me or to anyone in my family, and not to his mum either. Finding a convenient time to phone Australia is a nightmare even if he wanted to, which I doubt. He loves her but they've lived apart for too long now for her to feature much in his everyday life.

I sat opposite the doctor while he took my blood pressure and asked a few questions. We had been here before, Dr. Gove and I, so I knew all the right answers. I was wearing make-up too, and one of my nicer sweaters, and he noticed. Refusing the cup of coffee Ma offered to make him, he repacked his bag and stood up. "No problems that a change of scene won't put right," he said.

I gave him a grateful smile and saw his jowly old face twitch in unexpected complicity just before he turned to Ma. "Maybe you could babysit tonight Mrs. Pavalak, so Rachel and her husband can have a night out."

Babysitting is not my mother's thing, and with so many grandchildren who can blame her. Besides, I've nieces and nephews who are old enough to babysit if I want to go out, and despite their carping I know my sisters will look after Leah too, just as long as I don't ask too often. Besides, I wasn't sure I wanted to do as Dr. Gove had suggested. Ma wasn't about to let me argue with him though, so she just tightened her lips and nodded. He nodded too, and then I walked him to the door.

As he opened it he gave me another of his twitchy smiles, the ones that look more like a frown. "How's that husband of yours?"

I started to say he was fine but Dr. Gove heard the hesitation in my voice. He shook his head. "Let your mother babysit, Rachel."

Chapter Two

We couldn't decide between the local pub or a restaurant in town. Eventually we settled on the pub, mainly because of the price if I'm honest. Now I'm a stay-at-home mum we have to pay someone else to help out in the shop, which means we don't have a lot of spare cash. Not that we ever had that much anyway but in the days before Leah we could afford an occasional splurge.

"Are you sure your mother is fine about the babysitting?" Daniel asked as we walked into the village.

I nodded. "Thanks to Dr. Gove she couldn't say no."

He gave my hand a squeeze. "I didn't know you could be so evil Rach, not when you know how much she hates it."

I grinned at him. "It was an opportunity. Besides, she's been with me all day so another hour or two won't hurt her, and Pa says he'll collect a pizza on his way over."

He chuckled as he pushed open the door to the pub and followed me across to the bar. Tom, the owner, was in the middle of serving a customer, but he gave us a wide smile of welcome. As soon as he could he came over. "So he does let you out then. I was beginning to think he had chained you to Leah's crib. Welcome back, Rachel."

We laughed because we were expected to but I knew Daniel was upset. I couldn't tell Tom it had been me who refused to leave the house though, nor that Daniel had eventually stopped asking me to. That was private stuff, shameful even, and not something to be shared with Tom despite the fact I'd known him forever. Instead I pasted on my brightest smile. "We're celebrating getting our life back now that Leah sleeps through and has started to eat solids."

Pushing a foaming glass of beer towards Daniel, he gave a mock shudder. "Broken nights! Don't remind me. I'm glad I'm past all that."

As Tom's only daughter had been my best friend before she upped sticks and moved to London, I was surprised he could even remember. To change the subject, I asked him about Ella. By the time he had brought me up-to-date and told me she was coming down at the end of the month, Daniel had finished looking at the menu and was ready to order. I said I'd have chicken and chips, then changed to liver and bacon when I remembered Dr. Gove had told me to eat more red meat as I was borderline anemic.

"And what are you having to drink? The house red is good at the moment," Tom reached for a wine glass.

I shook my head. "I'm sticking with the soft stuff until I've stopped feeding Leah. I'll have an orange juice."

"Coming up just as soon as I've put your order through. Go and sit next to the fire and I'll bring your drink over in a minute."

We did as we were told and it was nice and cozy. Although it was late spring, the evenings were still chilly so the warmth was very welcome. Someone had recently put a log on the fire and orange and purple sparks were reflected in the dark shiny wood of the table. I sat on the bench and Daniel took the chair and we looked at one another. It felt odd to be out on our own after so long, and odder still to be tongue-tied. We were though. Daniel because he was still worried that if he said the wrong thing I'd snap his head off, and me because the only thing I wanted to talk about was the woman I had seen by Leah's crib, and talking about her was strictly off limits. I still hadn't let myself think about her. I was saving it for later, when I was on my own.

Not knowing what to say didn't matter though, because in less than a minute a man came over. He was tall and thin and his hands were knobbly with arthritis. I noticed them when he pulled a handful of coins from his pocket and put them on the table. "Buy yourself and your young lady a drink, my boy." His voice was rich and plummy and completely at odds with his down-at-heel appearance.

Without looking at the coins, which were not nearly enough for two drinks, Daniel smiled at him. "Thank you very much, Mr. Cullen."

14

"It's the least I can do because where would we all be without the village shop," the old man said. Then, with a brief nod in my direction, he shuffled back to his solitary half-pint of lager.

I gave Daniel one of my beady looks. He shifted uncomfortably in his chair. "He's an old man, Rachel, and he doesn't have anyone to look out for him."

"Except Saint Daniel," I knew I was being bitchy but I couldn't stop myself. Didn't want to stop myself. "How much does he actually owe you?"

"Not enough to make a fuss about. His pension didn't quite cover his groceries last month so I told him he could settle up later."

"Instead of which he pretends to buy you a drink," I said, pushing the coins towards him so hard that one tipped off the table onto the floor.

Daniel bent down and retrieved it. When he sat up again his eyes were sad. "His pride is all he has left, Rach."

"And pride will be all we have left if you carry on giving away our stock."

It was an old argument but one we hadn't had recently because I'd been too preoccupied with Leah and my own inner devils. Now I was feeling better I was quite capable of dredging up all my past grievances though, and I would have done if Tom hadn't arrived with my drink and a message from Ella. He said she had just phoned to say she couldn't make it after all but she would be down soon. She had sent her love and told him to tell me she was looking forward to catching up.

I smiled and said all the right things because I knew how much he was hurting even though he pretended it was fine that she had let him down yet again.

When Ella finished training as a make-up artist she took a temporary job in a nail bar and joked about how she was waiting for her big chance. When it finally arrived in the shape of a job on a film set, my free manicures stopped. What I hadn't expected was that our friendship would stop too. Well not stop exactly, more fade away. I mean how could I compete with someone who worked with celebrities every day and got to travel across the globe? Spag bol washed down with a couple of glasses of cheap wine at my kitchen table didn't really cut it, so it wasn't long before we were down to Christmas and birthday cards, and pretend hugs on the few occasions we actually did meet.

Of course I had Daniel and Leah whereas Ella was still single, and as far as I could tell, fancy free, although for all any of us knew, she was shacked up with some gorgeous celebrity and he was the reason she didn't come home any more.

Anyway, Tom's determination not to let us see how miserable he actually was, did the trick. Instead of being angry with one another, Daniel and I talked about Ella for the rest of the evening, and about what it must be like to work in film studios and on location in some of the most exotic places on earth. Actually I did most of the talking and Daniel did most of the listening but as that's how it's always been, except for the few weeks I was ill, it took us back to the years before Leah, the years when we couldn't get enough of one another, the years when the stockroom behind the shop sometimes saw activity we should have saved for the bedroom. For the first time in a long time I looked at Daniel, actually properly looked at him, and what I saw made my heart buck hard against my ribs.

Daniel's eyes locked with mine as he drained his glass and I knew his heart was racing too. It has always been the same with us, a look or a touch sparking a sudden need that is both scary and wonderful at the same time. Scary, because wanting another human being so much makes me fearful about a future without him, and wonderful because…well, it just is.

Without a word he held out his hand and I took it. He had already paid Tom, so we slipped out without saying goodbye, using the side door so we could avoid walking through the bar and having to stop to speak to people we knew. It felt like the times we had sneaked away from our friends before we were married, knowing they wouldn't notice until it was time for another round of drinks, and knowing, when they did, that we would be the butt of a few

16

ribald remarks before they returned to more important topics like football, music, or the latest reality show on TV.

When we reached the old willow tree on the edge of the village green we pushed past the branches that droop to the ground and slid into the dark, hidden space behind. We couldn't see a thing, but it wasn't important. Touch was enough, and words.

"I've missed this," Daniel whispered as he slid his hands beneath my bulky sweater and tried to unhook my bra.

I stopped his mouth with a kiss as I moved his hands round to the front fastener because I was still wearing a nursing bra. Elegant and sexy it wasn't but it did the job, and it was clear that Daniel was turned on by my fuller curves. I blush when I think what might have happened in the shadow of the willow tree if my milk hadn't decided to come in because, whatever my maternal deficiencies, lack of breast milk wasn't one of them, something I proved as I pressed my body against his. With a sigh he pulled my sweater down and took my hand. "Come on, let's go home. Leah's waiting for you."

I'm ashamed to say I had completely forgotten about Leah but she hadn't forgotten me. We could hear her crying before we unlocked the door and she was red with fury when Ma handed her to me. "I'm sorry, we should have come home sooner," I apologized as Leah latched hungrily onto my leaking breast.

Although she didn't say anything I could tell Ma was irritated and I understood why. After years of child-rearing and then helping out with too many grandchildren, the one thing she enjoyed was a quiet evening in front of the TV, a glass of wine in one hand and the remote control in the other. I kissed her cheek and then left Daniel to walk her and Pa to the door with more apologies. When he came back he stood and watched Leah and me for a moment, then he gave me a slow smile, the old sexy Daniel smile that did things to my pulse rate.

"I'll be in bed," he said.

I didn't need to answer.

Neither of us had reckoned on Leah though. She was usually so sleepy when she had her late night feed that I could put her back in her crib the moment she finished. Not this time. I had kept her waiting for so long that she refused to cooperate, plus her crying jag had given her hiccups. It took me ages to settle her, and when I finally crept from the nursery into the bedroom Daniel was asleep.

I stood and looked at him. He was lying on his front with his head turned away from me and one arm hanging over the side of the bed. The moonlight filtering in through the gap in the curtains painted silver stripes on his bare skin. He is beautiful, my husband, and part of me wanted to touch him, to wake him up and kiss him again, and do all the other things that we so nearly did under the willow tree. I didn't though. I told myself it was because it was late and he needed to be at the shop early for deliveries, but I was lying. It was because I was angry. Angry that he had fallen asleep while I was wrestling with Leah. Angry that he hadn't been able to stay awake for me.

I threw off my clothes and kicked them across the room. Then I climbed into bed and lay ramrod straight as far away from Daniel as possible. Ridiculous I know because he was fast asleep and oblivious. Then, because I was wide awake and alone with my thoughts, I did what I'd been putting off all day, I thought about the woman I'd seen beside Leah's crib that morning.

Despite everything, I hadn't wavered in my belief that she was real even though Daniel hadn't seen her when she was standing right in front of him. I knew it made no sense and something else was bugging me too. Although I had been too frightened to take in much about her, I had still registered she was different. What was it? Her hair, her dress, the way she moved? I rolled my head from side to side on the pillow, trying to recall how she looked. When I remembered I sat bolt upright. She had been wearing the sort of clothes I've only ever seen in history books; a long gray skirt with some sort of wide ribbon around the hem, and a white blouse with a high collar and long sleeves, and her dark hair had been twisted into an old-fashioned loose knot on the top of her head.

I almost woke Daniel until I remembered how he had looked right through her and then called Ma and Dr. Gove. No, I couldn't tell Daniel anything about her; not how she looked, nor how she had smiled at me, nor how she had…I suddenly went hot and cold all over as it hit me. Her funny little wave of farewell had very definitely said she would be back. I knew it as sure as if she had spoken to me. What I didn't know was why. What did she want from me? If it was Leah then I was going to have to persuade Daniel, and Ma and Dr. Gove that she was real and that we should talk to the police.

I lay back down again and stared at the gap in the curtains as I tried to work it out. The moon had been replaced by a pale gray sliver of light that told me dawn wasn't far off. I needed to grab at least a couple of hours sleep before Leah woke up or I'd be exhausted by lunchtime. I closed my eyes and started to count. Breath in for four… pause… breathe out for four… pause. It worked, eventually, and just before I drifted off I sent silent thanks to the nurse at Dr. Gove's surgery who had thrust a leaflet into my hand as I was leaving one day, and told me the local yoga class would do more for me than all the pills I was popping.

Chapter Three

Daniel was up, showered and dressed before I woke the following morning. He smiled down at me as I stretched and opened my eyes, screwed them up against the sunlight bursting in through the window, and shut them tight again.

"Hello, sleepyhead. All that crying wore Leah out last night. She's still dead to the world."

I wished he hadn't used the word dead, not when I still didn't know what the mystery woman wanted. With an effort I kept my voice casual as I hitched myself up and took the mug of tea he was holding out to me. "You've been in to see her then?"

"Of course I have, just like I do every morning. She's fine." He sat on the bed, his face creased into a frown. "Are you sure you're going to be alright today?"

I forced a smile, even though the look on his face irritated the hell out of me. "Of course I am. What was yesterday evening all about if it wasn't about me trying to get back to normal, even if you didn't quite manage to stay the course?"

It was a subtle dig but it was enough. He gave an embarrassed shrug "I was tired I guess, and Leah...well you know what Leah was like."

I knew only too well what Leah had been like because I'd been the one who had sat with her for over an hour while he snored himself into oblivion in the next room. I decided not to pursue it though. "Maybe we'll have more luck next time," I said in a bright and breezy voice, and then I drank my tea.

* * *

I stayed in bed until I heard the door slam and the roar of the ignition as Daniel put our battered old estate car into gear. As soon as the tires bit into the gravel I got up, and with a fast beating heart tiptoed into the nursery.

Leah was lying on her back with her head turned to one side. Her hair was a curly brown halo against the white sheet. I stared down at her, willing her to stay asleep for just a little longer so I could have a few more moments alone. With my big family all living locally, and our shop only just over a mile away in the centre of the village, I don't get much time on my own. Not that it usually bothers me but today I wanted some time to think and I wouldn't be able to do that once Leah was awake, nor when Ma called to check up on me as she was bound to do, or when Daniel phoned halfway through the morning on some pretext even though we would both know it was because he was checking up on me too.

Turning, I tiptoed out of the nursery, dropped my pajamas onto the floor beside the bed and walked naked into the bathroom. I showered quickly and then stood in front of the mirror and looked at myself. Apart from the blue milk veins in my breasts, what I saw wasn't bad. Somehow, without even trying, I had regained my figure, so my waist was slender again and my hips about the same size they had always been. My legs are good too, thanks to Ma's genes. Long and slim and cellulite free, they are probably my best feature.

I let my gaze travel upwards. I've never thought of myself as pretty but I know that good teeth and a straight nose are definite assets, as are green eyes and long brown lashes. My hair is okay too. Nothing to write home about but it's a pretty color, brown with some chestnut highlights and a natural curl. I keep it simple, the same as I keep my nails short, because I've never been a high maintenance sort of girl. I'm too practical for that, and too sporty. Well I was before Leah. Now a walk into the village had replaced my daily jog, and getting ready for my weekly yoga class took so much organization that I often felt like packing it in.

With a sigh, I toweled my hair dry. I still looked more or less the same as I always had so why didn't I feel the same? Had having Leah changed me in some undefinable way? Despite loving her so much it hurt, I still spent most of my life being angry. Ma said it was hormones but I didn't believe her. There was more to it than that but I couldn't figure out what it was.

Wrapped in a towel I trailed back into the bedroom and began to get dressed. I was halfway into my jeans when I heard a noise behind me. Swinging round I caught sight of a long gray skirt swishing through the door into the nursery. Without bothering to pull on a sweater I leapt across the bed and pushed the door wide, my heart hammering in my chest and my hands clammy with fear. I don't know what I expected to see but what I actually saw had me rooted to the spot. Leah was smiling up at the woman who, just like the previous morning, was leaning over her crib, only this time she was singing. I couldn't hear a thing but Leah clearly could because she kept gurgling with toothless delight. More to the point, she looked just the way she did when I sang to her.

It took me a moment to push the ridiculous feeling of jealousy from my mind. When I did, a mixture of fury and fear took over. "Why do you keep coming here?" I screeched, startling both of them, and making Leah cry.

The woman shook her head reprovingly as she bent over Leah again and said something that soothed her into smiles even though tears were still trickling down her face. Then she straightened up and looked at me and her eyes were full of…what? Compassion, concern, interest? I knew, in that instant, that Leah was safe, and that I was too. Whoever this woman was, she wasn't going to hurt us. I still wanted to know why she was here though, but before I could ask she switched on the mobile hanging above the crib, smoothed Leah's curls with a hand as tender and gentle as mine is when I'm overcome with love for her, and then she left as she had come, through the doorway into the bedroom.

Grabbing Leah, I followed her, but by the time we reached the bedroom, she had disappeared. I hurried to the window, expecting to see her walking away from the house but there was nobody there apart from John Tyler who used to sit next to me in school. He was leaning against the mail van smoking a cigarette. He saw me and waved. I put Leah on the bed while I pulled a sweater over my head, then picked her up again and made for the front door.

"Did you see a woman walk down the path just now?" I asked him as he dropped his cigarette butt and ground it out on the road with his foot.

He shook his head. "Not a soul."

"And you've been here for how long?"

He gave me an odd look. "As long as it takes to smoke a ciggie Rachel. Are you okay?"

I forced a smile because everyone around here knew I'd been ill and I didn't want him talking to my mother when he delivered her mail. "I'm fine, thanks. It's just that I'm expecting someone and I thought I heard a knock on the door while I was getting dressed."

He shrugged. "Must have been the wind. It's blowing up today. If you're thinking of going out, you'd better make it this morning because a storm is coming in later."

I thanked him and closed the door, wondering as I did so how many more lies I would have to tell before I discovered who the woman was.

I talked to Leah while I spooned stewed apple into her ever open mouth and then pushed up my sweater so she could guzzle milk until she was full. "Who is she, sweetheart?" I asked her. "And what does she want?"

Leah's only answer was a resonant burp that seemed much too big for such a small body. Then, of course, the inevitable happened, and I needed to change her diaper. After that I washed her face, dressed her and put her in her stroller. Then, ignoring the clothes on the floor and the unmade bed, I raked a finger through my own curls, brightened my face with lip gloss and mascara, and, slamming the door behind me, set off for the village.

I inhaled deeply as a playful breeze blew the scent of wild garlic into my nostrils. It was too nice a day to stay indoors doing housework. Besides, I had a plan.

* * *

Daniel was nowhere to be seen when I pushed open the door to the shop and maneuvered Leah inside. Instead, Millie Carter was standing behind the counter, bold as brass. She smiled when she saw me, that spiteful little smile that nobody else ever sees and which started on the day Daniel asked me to dance with him instead of her at the local disco.

"Feeling better today are you, Rachel? Daniel said you weren't too good yesterday. He was really worried about you but I suppose that's only to be expected when you've had such a rough time of it."

Underneath the sympathy I heard what she was really saying although to most people it probably sounded like genuine concern. She was telling me to be careful, that if I worried Daniel once too often he would look somewhere else for solace, and that when he did she would be waiting. It was something I worried about too on the rare occasions I stopped feeling sorry for myself, so it was why my tongue was sharper than usual.

"I'm fine. One off day isn't exactly the beginning of a major illness."

She came around the counter to look at Leah. Leah stared back at her through those dark eyes that are exactly like Daniel's. The dimple in her cheek is the same too. Only her hair is like mine, or at least it will be when it grows to more than a few wispy curls on the top of her head

"She's the spit of her daddy, isn't she?" I had to force myself not to jerk the stroller away when she bent close and made those stupid noises that pass for baby talk. Leah, however, was having none of it. Without me lifting a finger she went into total melt down, her screams ratcheting upwards until Millie backed away.

"Goodness she's got quite a temper, hasn't she?" She flushed slightly as she retreated behind the counter while I dangled my keys over the pram in an attempt to distract my angry daughter.

Although I wanted to award Leah five stars for picking up on my dislike in such a big way, I kept the satisfaction out of my voice when I asked Millie where Daniel was. She didn't keep the satisfaction out of hers when she told me though.

"He's in town all day today. First he's going to the wholesalers and then he has to see someone about getting some flyers made in time for the holiday season, and he said he has some sort of business meeting too."

Although I didn't have the first clue what she was talking about, I wasn't going to let her know that, so I just nodded wisely and made some excuse about having forgotten what day it was. I knew she didn't believe me but as she couldn't prove a thing I claimed another point on our virtual score board. My satisfaction didn't last however, not when I made the mistake of asking her how long she was filling in for Patsy, the cheerful middle-aged woman Daniel had taken on to replace me when I gave up working.

"Patsy left. Didn't he tell you? Her daughter is ill with something really nasty and she's gone off to look after the children."

Millie's long hazel eyes held a gleam of triumph as they met mine, and although the rational part of my mind could understand why Daniel hadn't told me about Patsy's daughter when I was so ill myself, the other part wanted to strangle him.

"So you're helping out until she comes back. That's nice of you Millie."

She shook her head as her mouth quirked into an amused smile. "Not helping out, Rachel. I work here. I've been working here for three weeks now…ten 'til three with half-an-hour for lunch. Daniel was great when I said the job would have to fit in with school hours."

I stared at her. So that was why Daniel had started leaving so early every morning. Someone needed to open up for the parents on the school run, the commuters on their way to the station, the 'up with the lark' dog walkers. It was all trade we couldn't afford to lose and when I was working we had always shared the early opening, and that had been the agreement with Patsy as well. She was someone we had both known since the days she had run the now defunct Post Office, so when she agreed to work for us we had been delighted. With Patsy in charge there would be nothing to worry about when Daniel wasn't there. Yet, without telling me, he had replaced her with someone I didn't like and who was taking him for a ride over what hours she was prepared to work. Worse, he hadn't even told me about Patsy's daughter. For the second time in ten minutes I wanted to kill my husband.

Taking my stunned silence for exactly what it was, Millie gave me another one of those smiles. "He didn't tell you, did he?"

When I shook my head, she tilted hers slightly sideways, finger to cheek. "I expect he didn't want to worry you, not with you struggling to cope and everything."

I shrugged as nonchalantly as I could and hoped she couldn't hear my teeth grinding together in anger. "It's not exactly an important decision is it, employing a part-time assistant? He probably just forgot."

It was a bit lame as retorts go but the spots of color on her cheeks told me the barb had struck home. I gave her a false smile. "I only called in to pick up some chocolates and a bottle of wine. Ma babysat yesterday while Daniel and I went out for a meal, so it's the least I can do."

Her face soured slightly and it was then that I remembered she was a single mum whose husband had left her three months after her youngest boy was born. She had been the first of all the girls at school to get married, the first to have children, and now she was the first to get divorced. Her parents were both dead too, so she didn't get to go out much at all what with the cost of babysitters and the fact that going out wasn't much fun unless you had someone to go out with. It was when I remembered her situation that I knew why Daniel had employed her. It was because he felt sorry for her and because he knew that a job that fitted in with school hours would make her life a whole lot easier.

I should have felt pleased about it; glad I was married to such a thoughtful man. Instead, all I felt was aggrieved, even if it was tinged with a slight feeling of guilt. As far as I was concerned Millie Carter's hard life was all of her own making…well not her parents being dead obviously…but the rest of it, and Daniel had no right to let her problems interfere with our life. He had let Millie snatch away his early mornings with Leah and me just so she could take her kids to school. The evenings too. No chance of him ever finishing early while Millie worked for him, not unless she let her children run riot in the shop.

"I'll take those," I pointed to a box of chocolates on the shelf behind her, my voice as neutral as I could make it. "And this looks okay." I plucked a bottle of white wine from the cooler.

She handed me the chocolates and told me the total cost, and then asked how she should put it through the till. I told her to talk to Daniel. As far as I was concerned he had employed her without saying a word to me, so he could explain the system when we took stuff from the shelves for our own use.

She nodded and then came around the counter to open the door for me. I maneuvered the pram out with a now sleeping Leah inside, all the while wishing she hadn't done that. I wanted to carry on feeling angry with her. I wanted to be able to tell Daniel he had made a mistake employing someone like her, someone who would need to take days off when one of her children was sick. I wanted ammunition to pick a fight with him. Instead, Millie made me feel a bit ashamed when she helped me maneuver the stroller down the step, which was why I smiled at her I guess. The warmth of her response startled me.

"Hang in there Rachel," she said. "It's tough at the beginning but it will get better, especially when you've got someone like Daniel to share it with."

* * *

I pondered her words as I pushed Leah through the village and then down the dusty track that led to the farm. Actually farm is a bit of an exaggeration, it's a smallholding really, with a few chickens and ducks, two goats, and an ancient horse who spends most of his time nodding sleepily under the apple tree and is no good for anything at all these days.

Long before I'd come to any conclusion about Millie's words, I reached the farmhouse. The kitchen door was wide open and a hen was pecking at some groundsel that was growing in a crack in the doorstep. Buffy, the border collie, whose main aim in life is to herd any child she sees into the barn, came running to meet me, her tail wagging. I pulled her ears, apologized for not having a biscuit in my pocket and parked the stroller in the shade. Leah was safe enough here because the farm was at least half a mile from the road, and anyway Buffy would bark if a stranger came into the yard. Anywhere else she would be in her baby carrier and strapped to me, asleep or not.

I could hear the laughter echoing around the kitchen before I stepped inside. Well, cackling really because Catherine, my second sister, is known for her ridiculous laugh. She makes the sort of screeching sound that would be funny if she wasn't related but as she is, it's just embarrassing. It's infectious though and she had obviously set Ma off and Rebecca, my youngest sister, who was there as well. I expected them to stop when they saw me, instead of which they all exploded into even more laughter.

"What...what?" I looked from them to the two boxes on the table and back again.

"Sorry love...it's just...you...it's..." Ma couldn't go on.

Catherine snorted as she rummaged in one of the boxes, found a photo and held it out to me. I stared at it. It was me at two years old wearing nothing but wellington boots and a ferocious scowl.

"Here's another one…and another one," She picked two more photos from the box and dropped them onto the table. I peered at them. They were more of the same. Me, the wellingtons and the scowl.

I could see I was cute. I could also see that the wellingtons added something, but I had no idea why Ma and my sisters found the photos quite so funny, and I said so.

"That's because you don't remember," Ma told me when she finally managed to compose herself. "You refused to wear clothes for most of that summer. As fast as I put them on you, you stripped them off, except for the wellies. You would have even worn those in bed if you could have gotten away with it."

"Do you remember when Aunt Jane came to visit?" Rebecca asked Ma and they all dissolved into splutters of laughter again. I could guess why without being told because Aunt Jane, who was actually Ma's cousin, was single, childless, and notoriously straight-laced. None of us could ever fathom why she bothered to visit the chaotic Pavalak household when all she did was tut and complain. Pa said it was because it made her feel superior. Ma said it was because she lived in the vain hope that one day we would listen to her and mend our ways. Only Daniel, on the two occasions he had met her since we got married, had wondered if it was because she was lonely. We had all scoffed him big time of course, and told him he wouldn't be so charitable if he had to put up with her visits every year. He nodded as if he took the point but when she visited last Christmas I noticed he spent quite a long time talking to her. They even took Buffy for a walk together.

I shrugged off the memory and began to rummage in the box of photos as the others continued to reminisce. Because I was so much younger there was a lot I didn't know about the family history, so I found the pictures of my sisters as babies almost as fascinating as the early ones of Ma and Pa.

As the youngest of the family I had grown up thinking I was the centre of the Pavalak universe. Until I was about five I'd found it inconceivable that the rest of the family had even had a life before I came along. Growing up had put paid to that of course and then, through my teenage years, I had been far too self-centered to pay much attention when they talked about the things that had happened before I was born. Now I had Leah it was different. I wanted to know everything so I could tell her about her family and answer her questions when she was old enough to start asking them.

I had managed to unearth baby pictures of two of my other sisters, one of Hannah in a fluffy all-in-one Babygro, and one of Ruth lying on a rug under the old apple tree at the top of the orchard, and was listening to Ma trying to remember when they were taken, when my heart almost stopped. I waited until I was sure I could control the expression on my face, and be sure that my voice wouldn't be wobbly, then I held out the photo I had just picked up.

"Who is this?" I asked ever so casually.

Instead of answering, Ma almost snatched it out of my hand. "That's what I've been looking for. That and ones like it. Which box did it come from Rachel?"

Catherine peered over her shoulder. "Is that a photo of Grandma when she was young?"

Ma shook her head. "No, it's a picture of her grandmother. You can tell by the clothes she's wearing that it's from a much earlier period."

Catherine nodded as she looked more closely. "I remember seeing a picture of her in Grandma's house when I was small. It was on the mantle and there was one of her grandfather too, although I can't remember what he looked like."

Ma's eyes softened. "Apparently he was quite a looker when he was young. Somewhere there's a photo of him wearing a straw boater and sporting a very dashing moustache."

"But what is her name?" I tried not to sound impatient. I didn't want to draw attention to myself in case my agitation triggered some sort of maternal warning in Ma, but I had to know.

She handed the photo back to me. "Rose, her name is Rose."

Rebecca looked pensive. "She's the one Grandma always refers to as Granny Rose isn't she?"

Ma nodded. "Yes. When she was small she used to spend a lot of time with her even though Rose was quite poorly by then. I think she had some sort of thyroid problem that would probably be easy to treat nowadays."

The conversation became another reminiscence as Catherine and Rebecca recalled their own childhood and Ma talked about the early days of her marriage to Pa when she'd only had a couple of children to care for, but I had stopped listening. All I could do was stare at the photo of Rose...my Rose...the woman who had been standing beside Leah's crib just a few hours earlier.

Chapter Four

It took me about ten minutes to ask the question I should have asked in the first place. "Why do you want pictures of Rose?"

"Because the nurses at Grandma's nursing home say photos of her own childhood, and of her parents and grandparents, will help her hold onto some of her memories for a bit longer."

I stared at her. Grandma was Ma's mother and she had begun to show signs of dementia a few years ago, soon after Grandpa died. At first she had just been a bit forgetful but when she started doing things like leaving the kettle boiling on the stove while she went shopping, and forgetting to eat, then we all knew she needed to be looked after.

There are enough of us that it should have been possible for her to move in with someone in the family but sadly it wasn't as simple as that. Ma tried at first but Grandma couldn't cope with the continuous stream of visitors. Nor could she cope with the volume of noise that a conversation between even two members of the Pavalak family entailed, so in the end she went into the nursing home. For the first week we thought she'd be heartbroken and we all felt guilty, but she took to it like a duck to water.

Within days she seemed to have forgotten she had ever lived anywhere else, and Hester, who has always been the bossy one, set up a family visiting rota, so that rarely a day goes by without one or other of us calling in to see her. She likes that, mainly because we take her chocolate biscuits and wine. Even at ninety-four years old she is still partial to a glass of chardonnay at six o'clock.

Ma went back to rummaging through the photos. "If I can find enough pictures of her and her family when she was young I can stick them all into an album and then we'll have something to talk about when we visit."

I started picking through the photos as well and when I saw the sepia print I felt my breath hitch in my chest. It was Rose again, only younger, and this time she was laughing. Actually she was more than laughing, she was the centre of attention, and whatever she was saying was making the other people in the photo laugh too. There were seven or eight of them, all sitting or kneeling on the ground as if it was some sort of picnic even though I couldn't see any food. Only Rose was standing, Rose and a tiny golden-haired girl of about four years' old who was wearing a ruffled dress. Rose was wearing a high-necked white blouse and a skirt with a dark ribbon around the bottom. I knew it was grey and that the ribbon was black because it was what she had been wearing when she stood beside Leah's crib earlier that morning.

Eventually I found my voice. "This is Rose again, isn't it?"

Ma leaned across the table and peered at the photo. "Yes, that's the photo I was talking about earlier, and that's your great-great-grandfather." She pointed to a young man wearing light colored trousers and a striped blazer. He had a straw boater tilted forwards on his head and his eyes were fixed on Rose. Below his very dashing moustache his mouth was full of laughter.

Rebecca grabbed the photo. "Wow, he was really handsome."

Suddenly I had a brainwave. "Let me sort out the photos and put them all in an album for you, Ma. I'd like to do that, and I'd like to talk to Grandma about them, too."

From the silence that followed my suggestion you'd have thought I'd grown two heads. In the end Ma spoke while my two sisters just stared at me.

"Are you sure, Rachel? Do you…will you be able to find the time, what with Leah and everything?"

"I'm quite sure," I said as firmly as I could. Then, because I thought I'd better give them a reason for my uncharacteristically generous offer before they began to wonder if I was beginning to take leave of my senses again, I added, "It will take me out of myself and give me something to do in the evening when Leah is asleep."

"In that case be my guest," Ma began to pile the photos back into the boxes. "I'll ask Pa to bring these over when he gets home, and when you've finished sorting through them we'll go to the nursing home together and show them to Grandma."

I smiled at her. "I'd like that." Then Leah started to cry and I didn't have to say anything else at all.

* * *

When Daniel arrived home I was sitting at the kitchen table surrounded by photos. Leah was already fast asleep in her crib. He bent and kissed my cheek.

"You look busy."

I nodded, too distracted to explain because I'd just spied another photo of Rose and it had sucked all the breath out of me. In this one she was a smaller, older, more faded version of the woman in the earlier photos. Although I was sure it was her, the merry smile had gone and so, too, had the carelessly upswept hair that spilt exuberant curls over her temples. Worse, the confident tilt of her head had gone as well. This was a photo of a careworn woman fast approaching middle age. I stared at it. Had she been ill when it was taken?

Daniel peered over my shoulder, his fingers warm on the nape of my neck. "Who's that?"

I fidgeted him away, too immersed in what I was doing to want to talk about it. "It's a photo of my great-great-grandmother."

When I failed to elaborate he tried another question. "Where did all these photos come from? I don't remember seeing them before."

"Ma gave them to me. I said I'd sort through them for her."

Although he would have had to be deaf to miss the dismissal in my voice, he didn't give up. Instead he picked up the photo album Ma had sent over with the boxes, and opened it. Seeing the blank pages, he added two and two together and made five. "She'll enjoy having pictures of all her family in one place."

As Ma had pictures of every member of the Pavalak family displayed all over the house, I knew the last thing she would ever want would be more of them gathered together in an album. It was the reason so many of them were all jumbled together in cardboard boxes, and it was also why I'd never seen most of them. I didn't bother to explain it to Daniel though, not when he was being so patronizing. I added the latest photo of Rose to the small pile I'd already put to one side and then tumbled the rest back into the boxes. By the time I'd finished, Daniel had boiled the kettle and made a mug of tea for each of us.

As I sipped mine I realized, with a guilty start, that I hadn't given a thought to our evening meal. Daniel was ahead of me, which wasn't difficult given that there were no pans on the hob and no cooking smells coming from the stove.

"Shall I do some pasta or would you prefer cold meat and salad? We could have it with the baguette I brought home. A few minutes in the cooker will freshen it up." He pointed to the long white paper bag on the kitchen counter and I knew at once that the loaf was past its sell by date, or at least it would be by the next day. For some reason it riled me.

"It would be nice, just for once, to tear pieces off a really fresh loaf instead of using up other people's left overs," I snapped.

He turned away so I couldn't see the expression on his face as he opened the fridge and began to pull out the ingredients to make a salad. Actually I didn't need to see his face to know it would be patient and long suffering and just a little bit hurt...not a lot hurt because Rachel was still not quite herself so she couldn't help behaving like a bitch at times. Of course he wouldn't ever have called me a bitch, even to himself. I knew I was being one though and after a moment's reflection I knew why.

"How long has Millie Carter been working at the shop?" Although I tried to keep my voice casual it had an edge to it.

He sighed as he switched on the stove. "She said you came in today."

"When were you going to tell me?"

"When you start listening, Rachel."

His words took me by surprise and for a moment I was silent. He turned and looked at me. "I've had to make a lot of decisions since Leah was born, decisions we would have shared once upon a time. Employing Millie was one of them, and her need was as great as mine."

"You mean when Patsy left in a hurry and you forgot to tell me about that, too."

His eye's darkened to black, a sure sign he was getting angry. "I didn't forget to tell you. I decided you didn't need to know about her daughter's illness when you were still so poorly yourself."

I picked up the stale baguette and placed it on the top shelf of the stove. "Well I'm not poorly now, so you can include me in all your decision making in future, and we can start by revising Millie's hours."

He ripped open a pack of cold meat, something he had brought home from the shop the previous evening but which we hadn't eaten because we'd gone out instead. "Listen to yourself Rachel, and then tell me honestly whether you want to be that unkind…you, who has sisters and a mother at your beck and call whenever you need help, and a husband too, god help him."

The last remark was muttered under his breath but I heard it and it made everything spill over into a stream of invective I wasn't proud of. By the time I'd finished complaining about his selfishness and how he was putting Millie Carter's needs before Leah and me in the mornings, I almost believed it. I think Daniel gave up listening before I was halfway through, which was probably a good thing, and by the time I had enough sense to shut up, the salad was ready and so was the bread.

We didn't have much to say to one another after that. I didn't ask him about his day, and he didn't ask about mine. We washed the dishes in silence too and then he spent the rest of the evening going through the month's accounts while I returned to the photos.

My heart wasn't in it however, and when Leah stirred for her night feed I hurried through to the nursery, glad to have something else to do. I didn't expect Rose to be there because for some reason I'd persuaded myself she was an early morning apparition. I was wrong but this time she didn't smile when she saw me. She just looked sad. Then, while I was still wondering why seeing her no longer frightened me, she slipped past me and out of the door.

I half expected to hear Daniel speak to her but he didn't. Instead he turned on the TV, and when I joined him, after I had settled Leah back into her crib, he was watching the highlights of a football game. There was a glass of whiskey on the table beside him which I knew meant he was going to stay up late and that it was my fault. For a moment I considered snuggling up beside him on the sofa and trying to persuade him that deep down I was still the Rachel he had married, but then I shrugged. If that was how he wanted to play it then I was going to bed. If he was determined to do all the early starts to make life easy for Millie Carter, then I needed all the sleep I could get.

Chapter Five

Daniel left earlier than usual the following morning. Although he kissed me like he always did, I knew it was just from habit, not because he wanted to. It made me mad all over again even though deep down I knew I deserved it. To take my mind off how I felt I pulled out the box of photos as soon as Leah had finished her breakfast. I should have washed and dressed her, but she seemed perfectly happy watching me from her bouncy chair, and she grinned gummily whenever I spoke to her. I spoke to her a lot.

"Look at this one, Leah. This is a picture of your great-great-great-grandma when she was younger than me. She was pretty, wasn't she? As pretty as you are going to be when you grow up."

By the time Leah was ready for her morning nap we had been through the whole box, and the small pile of old family photos I had picked out the previous evening had grown considerably. At first I had only looked for pictures of Rose but then I decided to include all those other pictures of people in period dress. People I knew nothing about but who, with luck, might trigger those parts of Grandma's memory that hadn't yet succumbed to the cruel ravages of dementia.

By the time Daniel came home that evening I had finished the album, and because I was feeling so pleased with myself I had kept Leah up so she could spend some time with her daddy while I cooked the supper. The smile that lit up Daniel's face when he found us both in the kitchen waiting for him twisted the little knife of guilt I'd been harboring in my heart all day, and when he kissed us both it twisted just a little bit more. I thrust Leah at him.

"Now you are having to leave so early in the mornings, I've decided to keep her up a bit later in the evenings so she can see you before she goes to sleep."

I wasn't getting at him. My decision to keep Leah up had far more to do with my guilt than with our recent argument about Millie Carter, but he still reacted. I saw the tension in his shoulders and the sudden hardening of his jaw as he settled Leah into a more comfortable position. I decided to ignore it. Nothing good would come of trying to explain myself. Instead I made him a mug of tea, checked that the chilli beef I was cooking was bubbling away at the right temperature, and then followed him into the sitting room and told him about the album.

"Leah was in charge of all the decision making," I said. "She directed the whole project from her chair. I only used the photos she approved of and I abided by her rule of no more than four per page maximum. She's going to be a real taskmaster when she grows up."

He grinned at me, the old Daniel grin that once upon a time would have had me wondering if I should turn off the stove and make for the bedroom, or whether it would be better to eat first and then spend the rest of the evening in bed. Having Leah had changed all that of course but it was good to know I remembered, and from the expression on his face, Daniel did too.

Resting Leah securely on his knee so that he could take a sip of tea from his mug, he spoke to her. "So you're a chip off the old block, are you? An organizer like your mother."

I nodded as I put the album on the sofa next to him, enjoying our silly conversation because it meant we were back on track again. "She's a real slave driver. It would have taken me days to do this by myself."

He drained his mug and put it on the floor beside the couch. "We'd better look at it then hadn't we, young lady? Come on, I'll turn the pages and you can tell me who all these strange looking people are."

Leah, enjoying the attention, gurgled contentedly as he propped her on a cushion beside him so they could both look at the album. I stood behind the sofa and watched as he turned the pages, wondering how much Grandma would remember about her childhood, wondering how much she would remember about Rose.

39

* * *

At that point the evening had potential. Daniel put Leah to bed while I finished cooking the supper and later, when we'd eaten and I was washing dishes at the sink, he put his arms around me and nuzzled my neck the way he knew I liked it. It had the effect it always did. As he kissed the soft skin where my neck joined my shoulder something shifted inside me. It was a sort of blooming so that every bit of me became receptive to his touch. I turned in his arms, my hands still wet with suds, and kissed him. It was a kiss that would have gone on for a very long time and might have ended up in the bedroom if my sister Hannah hadn't rapped on the outer door before letting herself into the porch.

With a sigh of frustration, I left Daniel to finish the dishes while I went to greet her. She was wearing her usual harassed look, the one that said I'm your sister and you've been ill so I have to check on you even though I have a list of far more important things to do. Her concerned smile was genuine though.

"How are you? How is Leah? Ma said you had a bit of a setback while I was away."

Hannah is the clever one in the family. She's a pediatric consultant and she is always attending conferences somewhere or other, leaving her own children to bring themselves up. Ma used to complain about it when they were small but now they're older she leaves them to get on with it.

I returned her smile. I knew she had come for all the right reasons and I know, too, how shitty her life is. While she works all hours, her husband stays at home waiting for the muse to strike. This means he has a pile of unpublished manuscripts on the corner of his desk as well as a body odor problem because he wears the same T-shirt day after day. Ostensibly a house-husband, he neither cooks nor cleans, and he only communicates with his children when he absolutely has to. This means both boys spend most of their spare time in their bedrooms playing computer games amid a suppurating mess of dirty socks, sweaty gym kits and the crumbs from left-over pizzas.

"I'm fine. I think I was probably sleep-walking or something and I woke up a bit too suddenly," I lied. "If it had been you or anyone else, nobody would have taken any notice, but because it was me, Daniel and Ma worried I was becoming paranoid again."

I was surprised at the expression of relief that swept across her face. She really did care; she wasn't just being dutiful. Another wave of guilt pierced me as I remembered the times I had complained about her to Daniel, saying she should spend more time at home sorting out her own life instead of interfering in ours. He had taken her side of course, saying she was just worried about Leah and that as soon as I was well enough to care for her full time then she would stop calling so often. Now, seeing how tired she looked, and seeing the sadness that was always a shadow in the back of her eyes, I forgot I had ever resented her.

"Come in and have a glass of wine, or there's coffee if you'd rather. I was just about to make some anyway." I pushed open the door to the sitting room.

For a moment she hesitated, then she nodded. "I'd love to. I'm sure Paul and the boys can manage without me for another hour or so."

The truth was that when she did go home she would be lucky if any of her menfolk even looked up from whatever they were doing. She knew it and she knew I knew it, so we changed the subject, talking instead about Leah. When Daniel joined us he asked her about the conference she had just been to and we talked about that for a bit too. Then, searching for something else that wouldn't bring us back to her own family, I remembered the photo album and fetched it. It was news to her because she hadn't seen Ma or any of my sisters for a week or so, but as soon as she saw what I'd done she was enthusiastic.

"What a lovely idea. I remember reading about something like this in one of the medical journals a few years ago."

"So you think it will work? You think it will help her to remember things about her own childhood, things about Granny Rose?" I tried to keep the excitement out of my voice.

She nodded thoughtfully. "It might do because very long term memories are usually the last to go. It's worth a try anyway," she started leafing through the album until she got to a photo of a church with a bridal party gathered outside. It was such a small picture that it was almost impossible to pick out individual people. I didn't think it had anything to do with Rose because the dress was early twentieth century. I had only stuck it in the album in case there was someone in it that Grandma had known in her youth.

Hannah pointed to it. "This is a picture of Grandma's wedding. Look, there's her sister all decked out as a bridesmaid, and there's her Uncle Robert giving her away because by then her father was dead."

I shifted across to sit next to her and peered to where she was pointing. The tiny black and white figures were almost undecipherable unless you knew who was there.

"How come you recognize it?"

"Because Grandma used to have a much larger version in her sitting room when I was a little girl. And look, there's Grandma's mother, and I think that old lady next to her is Granny Rose. I guess the other couple are the parents of the groom."

I'd lost interest in the tiny picture, however. I was intent on tracking down the larger one. "Where do you think it is now?"

My sister shrugged. "No idea. Grandma took it down years ago, once we all started to overload her with photos of her great-grandchildren. It's probably in that old chest of drawers in the barn, unless someone threw it out when we cleared the furniture from her bungalow."

I knew I'd be rummaging through that chest of drawers first thing the following morning when I took the photo album to show Ma. I didn't say that to Hannah though.

Instead I asked her what else she could remember about the early days of Grandma's life.

"Not a lot although I do remember her saying her grandmother used to play the church organ. It was quite odd actually. I'd just taken a psychology exam and when I told her about it, she was quite scathing. She said that in her day people found other ways to cope with unhappiness instead of talking about it all the time. Then she sort of implied that playing the organ somehow made her grandmother's life bearable. Now I know better I wish I'd asked her more about it, but I was a young 'know it all' medical student in those days so I just dismissed it as outdated rubbish."

Something shifted deep inside me. Was that why I was so bad tempered all the time? Did I need something to take me out of myself the same way that Hannah needed her tiny, intensive care babies and the children with heart murmurs and leukemia to make her life bearable? She filled every one of her waking hours caring for them and trying to save them and I suddenly realized it was so she didn't have to think about her shitty home life and her failing marriage. I didn't say it of course. Instead I poured her a second glass of wine while I wondered what it was that Rose was running away from when she played the organ.

* * *

Leah started moaning for her ten o'clock feed just as Hannah was getting up to leave, so of course she stayed a bit longer to check her out. Watching me lift her from the crib she smiled. "You've done it Rachel. Despite everything you've been through you've got Leah into a secure routine and she's thriving. Look how content she is. She knows she has to go straight back to sleep as soon as she's finished."

Praise indeed. My pediatric consultant sister telling me I was doing something right. I could feel myself swelling with pride even as she bent and kissed first me and then Leah, and tiptoed from the room. As I shifted into a more comfortable position, taking care not to disrupt Leah's sleepy suckling, I heard her say goodnight to Daniel, and a moment later the glare of headlights swept across the dimly lit nursery.

For once Daniel was still awake when I finally made it to the bedroom but by then neither of us had the energy to pick up where we'd left off. Instead we talked softly about Hannah, and about Grandma, until our eyelids began to droop.

Chapter Six

I was up with the lark next morning, all fired up with my plans. I concentrated on getting through the morning's chores as swiftly as possible. Leah was full of smiles and gurgles when I dressed her. She didn't even make her usual objection when I changed her diaper but just listened while I carried out our usual one-sided conversation.

"You're curious too, aren't you? You want to know more about the pretty lady who visits us. Well we might be lucky today but you mustn't tell anyone that you've seen her, not when they start talking about the photos. Not a word Leah, or they'll think we're both stark raving mad."

She beamed at me around the fingers she had stuffed in her mouth. I laughed. "Nobody will understand a word you say if you do that, so we're safe. Come on, let's go visiting."

It was only as we left the house that I realized Rose hadn't visited us that morning.

* * *

We went to the farm first so I could show Ma the album as well as search through the old chest of drawers that had been stored in the barn ever since Grandma sold her bungalow. Ma was eating her breakfast when we arrived. A lie-in and a late breakfast were the two things she loved most about retirement, not that she had ever had a career to retire from. She hadn't had time to work, not with seven daughters spread across twenty years and then a rapidly expanding tribe of grandchildren. Saying she had retired had nothing to do with employment. It was her way of embracing the empty nest syndrome with relish and making the most of every moment the house was empty. It was why she peered at me over the morning paper with less than her usual enthusiasm.

"You're up and about bright and early."

I blamed Leah without a qualm. Then I put the photo album on the table. Ma looked at it in surprise. "You've finished it already."

I nodded. "I enjoyed doing it and now I want to know who all these people are and whether they are relatives."

She flicked through the pages. "I recognize some of them but there are a lot of people I don't know, people who died before I was born. I wonder if Grandma will remember them."

"I thought we could go and see her today and show her the album."

Ma shook her head. "I'm meeting Louise at eleven and we're going into town but you can go if you want to."

Louise is my fifth sister, the one who likes buying things and whose husband has some sort of complicated job in a merchant bank that finances her shopping habit. She and Ma were obviously going to indulge in a bit of joint retail therapy. I felt a surge of excitement. Without Ma listening I could ask Grandma all the questions I wanted. I played the dutiful daughter though. "You won't mind if I show her the pictures without you being there?"

"Of course not. She will love to see you and Leah anyway, and if you can get her to look at the photos and talk about them, then that will be a bonus."

"I'll go then," I kept my voice casual. "Before I do though, I'm going to have a quick look in the old chest of drawers in the barn, just in case there's anything else stored away that might help."

* * *

I left Ma and Leah bonding over a crust of toast and hurried across the yard to the barn. Because it was the place where we all stored the things we no longer wanted but which we weren't quite ready to throw away or sell, its contents were a jumble of mismatched furniture, sports gear, bags of old clothes and a whole lot of baby stuff that I had refused to take. I worked my way through it, pushing bags and boxes out of the way until I found the chest of drawers right at the back behind some plastic sacks full of old duvets and pillows.

It took me a while to clear enough space so I could pull open the drawers but when I did the effort proved worthwhile because inside was a treasure trove of memories. I searched around the barn until I spied an old shopping trolley and quickly filled it.

Ma stopped singing to Leah when I trundled it into the kitchen behind me. "What on earth have you got in there?"

"A whole lot of things. Look." I lifted out a battered jewelry box, a bible, several photos in frames and more than a dozen faded notebooks filled with neat handwriting. There were also several pieces of wood shaped like feet without toes, a set of false teeth with very red gums, and a brightly painted ornament that looked for all the world like a very overweight pixie.

Ma laughed as she picked it up. "Goodness, is he still here? I thought Grandma had finally got rid of him."

"Why didn't she? He's very ugly."

"You know that and I know that, but Grandma would never have a word said against him. Her grandfather won it for her at the fair when she was a little girl and she's always loved it."

Her grandfather. "That would be Granny Rose's husband wouldn't it?"

"Yes, your great-great-grandfather. He was called Arthur."

"And what about these?" I indicated the rest of the stuff on the table, swiftly moving one of the wooden feet out of Leah's reach as she made a grab for it.

Ma stared at them. "I can't imagine why she kept those. Only a museum would want something like that."

I frowned as my hand caressed the smooth silkiness of the polished wood. "I don't even know what they are."

"They're cobbler's lasts...copies of people's feet really. The one you're holding is an ordinary one but some of these others are different. Look at this one. It's tiny. It must have belonged to a child. And that one over there has a peculiar bump in it as if its owner had a deformed foot. These must be individual lasts that either belonged to wealthy customers or to people who needed special shoes to help them walk."

"So Arthur made shoes."

"Yes, he was the village cobbler and very skilled I believe. According to Grandma he could take a shoe that was so worn out it was little more than a scrap of leather and repair it until it looked like new."

I picked up the tiny wooden last. It wouldn't be long before Leah's feet were as big as that. I felt a catch in my throat as I thought of it. This was a model of a real child's foot and I would never know whether it was a boy or a girl, or what color the shoes were that my great-great-grandfather had made. Now I had someone else I needed to find out about as well. Arthur, Rose's husband.

* * *

It was almost eleven o'clock by the time Leah and I arrived at the nursing home. The nurse who let me in gave me a running commentary as we walked down the corridor towards Grandma's room. It included the state of Grandma's bowels, how much she had eaten for breakfast and the fact that she seemed more alert than usual.

"Great, because I've brought some photos for her to look at," I said.

"She'll like that, and she will like seeing this one too," the nurse ruffled Leah's hair. "Babies and dogs, we need more of them visiting because they always cheer us all up."

"I'll bring Leah into the dining room when it's time for lunch so everyone can see her," I promised.

With a smile of approval, she whisked away in answer to a bell from another room, leaving me to it. The door was already open and Grandma was sitting in her usual chair by the window, the one Pa had taken over in the trunk of his car and then tried to carry in without asking for help. I couldn't remember a time when she had sat on anything else and it was the only thing she had insisted on taking with her when she moved. Its stuffing had molded itself to her shape over the years and she flatly refused to have it recovered and plumped up.

"It'll see me out," was one of her favorite phrases about almost everything she owned, and she said it about the chair most days.

She didn't hear Leah and me enter the room because she was too intent on the birds pecking at the crumbs outside her window. The bird feeder had been Daniel's idea. He had seen it at the wholesalers when he was stocking up on supplies for the shop and brought it home together with a huge bag of birdseed. He had taken both of them to the care home and set the feeder up outside grandma's window. Ma had been reduced to tears when she saw it, and tears weren't something she indulged in very often, not in public anyway.

"Only Daniel," she kept saying between sniffs. "The rest of us have been too busy feeling sorry for ourselves to think of ways to make things better for her."

"That's a bit harsh, Ma," Ruth said. "Look how lovely her room is. You and Pa have worked hard to make it a home-from-home for her. You've put up pictures and added cushions and some of the ornaments she loved and it all looks cozy and familiar."

"Except she isn't interested in familiar anymore, is she?" Ma said sadly. "She's forgotten where most of the things came from. She's even forgotten where she used to live for goodness sake, but the one thing she hasn't forgotten is how much she loved her garden and how the birds used to wait by the bird feeder every morning."

"I suppose so," Ruth said reluctantly, and I knew why. She wished she had thought of it or, more specifically, that

49

her husband had. More than anything though she wished it had been anyone but Daniel, because she didn't want to have to feel grateful for anything else. You see, Daniel was the one who bailed her out the time she bought a new dress instead of the weekly groceries and then was too frightened to tell her husband. I remember the look of relief on her face when he filled a couple of bags and loaded them into her car, telling her she could pay for them when she had sorted herself out. That had been when I was still working of course, so subbing her hadn't been much of a problem, not when we were didn't have to pay an assistant's wage out of our profits.

She paid us back in installments over the next few weeks and we had more or less forgotten about it until it happened again. This time she asked Daniel outright for some help instead of mumbling and sobbing like she had the first time. He gave her what she wanted and then he did the other thing she asked, and didn't mention it to me. Later, when I found out, he said he hadn't wanted to cause a family row and anyway what did a few tins of beans and a loaf of bread matter when he knew she would pay us back. She didn't though, so the third time she asked he was less understanding. Oh, he still let her have the food she needed and he gave her a bottle of wine too, but he also let her know what he thought of her extravagance.

"You can't keep doing this, Ruth," he said. He said a whole lot more too, about how we couldn't afford to keep subbing her and how she owed it to her husband to tell him she was struggling to manage on the money he gave her. It was a fair comment because her husband expected her and their teenage children to be perfectly turned out at all times, the same as he expected Ruth to entertain his clients and accompany him to company dinners, but all without giving her the funds she needed. Instead he spent his money on whatever was the latest 'must have' status symbol while the rest of the family pretended not to notice that he never bought a round of drinks or that none of us were ever invited around to their house for a meal.

I don't know whether Ruth did talk to her husband, or what he said if she did, but she never asked us to bail her out again, and she was never quite as friendly, either. Being beholden to people who know your secrets is difficult, so when Daniel erected the birdfeeder outside Grandma's window and it reminded her how much nicer he was than her own husband, she didn't like it.

It reminded me, too, as I pushed Leah across to where Grandma was sitting. I started talking about the birds before she could see me because I didn't want to startle her. The feeder was full and there were fresh crumbs on the windowsill. I knew that was due to Daniel, too, because one of the caregivers had told Ma he dropped by every morning on his way to work to check on them. I guess it was where a lot of the stale bread from the shop went as well. Daniel never mentioned it though, and nor did I. Now, seeing the pleasure on my grandmother's face as she watched a fat pigeon greedily clearing up the crumbs outside her window, I thought perhaps I should. In a line-up with all my sisters' husbands he would win hands down. I resolved to tell him so when I got home, to make up for how mean I had been recently.

* * *

"Hello Grandma, I've brought Leah to see you," I told her when I had her full attention.

She beamed at me. "You were always such a good girl, Molly. Come and sit beside me and tell me whose baby you are looking after today."

My heart sank. Who was Molly? I thought the nurse had said it was a good day. "It's Rachel Grandma, and Leah's my baby. Mine and Daniel's. When she wakes up you can hold her if you like."

She patted my hand. "Of course you're Rachel. Did I say you were someone else?

51

I shook my head. "It doesn't matter. We all look so much alike that I'm not surprised you get a bit muddled at times."

Her faded eyes suddenly sharpened as a particular memory came flooding back, although she struggled to voice it. "Not alike, no. Rachel isn't like Molly...or...no...Rachel is like Rose."

I stared at her, not quite able to believe what I was hearing. I'd never heard her mention Rose before, or Molly, whoever she might be, so why was she doing so now? I tried to conjure up the picture of the merry, dark-haired girl I'd seen in the sepia photograph but I couldn't. I couldn't see the shadowy woman who visited Leah in the morning either. The thought prompted me into remembering why I was there. I laid the album on her lap.

"I've brought you some photos to look at. I'd love it if you could tell me who the people in them are."

At first I thought she wasn't interested. It was only when she started to pluck ineffectually at the cover that I realized she didn't know how to open it. It shocked me for a moment. My Grandma had forgotten how to open a photo album. My Grandma who, once upon a time, had read the newspaper from cover to cover every day and who, when the rest of us started to buy most of our books over the Internet, still insisted on making her weekly visit to the local library. Then I realized it was the size and unfamiliarity of the album that was the problem and my world tilted back on its axis again as I leaned forward and turned to the first page.

Grandma stared at the pictures for so long that I began to despair. It wasn't going to work. She was beyond recognizing anyone, beyond remembering names. I was never going to find out anything about Rose. I was just about to prompt her, hoping to stir a long forgotten memory, when she spoke.

"That's Molly," she said, pointing to the tiny golden-haired girl in the photo I'd pasted on the first page. "She was such a good little girl, always helping her Mama with the baby."

52

I knew I had to tread carefully if I wasn't to distract her. Ma told me ages ago that when we asked Grandma questions, it confused her. She said it was best to try to join in with her conversation rather than make her listen to ours. I wasn't sure she was right but I thought I would try it anyway.

"She probably enjoyed looking after the baby more than playing with her dolls."

She shook her head and the glint of anger in her eyes surprised me. "She had to do it, even on schooldays if her Mama was poorly."

"Poorly?" I prompted when her voice tailed off in confusion.

There was another silence, then she carried on talking as if she had never paused. "When her Mama had headaches she had to go to bed."

"And that's when Molly had to look after the baby?"

Her eyes filled with tears. "Yes, and she was frightened when he cried and she couldn't wake her Mama up."

Panicking that I was about to upset her, I did the only thing I could think of, and turned the page. "Look, here's another picture." I pointed to a small photo of two little girls.

It was like the sun coming out from behind the clouds. "That's Joyce and Molly. They're playing in Auntie May's garden."

I was getting lost with all these names and she still hadn't told me who Molly was. Her sudden change of mood was confusing too. Was this a picture of Molly before there was a baby to look after? I peered at the photo hoping to find some sort of clue. Grandma beat me to it.

"Molly is wearing a blue frock."

I stared at the small black and white print, my heart beating fast. How did she know it was blue? This was going to take a long time, and deciphering Grandma's memories was going to be a struggle, but at least it seemed to be working. The photos were triggering memories long forgotten by her and not known to the rest of us.

"Was it a pretty frock?"

53

"Rose didn't like it."

My heart leaped when she mentioned Rose again. "Why not?"

"Because Aunt May sent it over even though she knew Rose wanted Molly to have a new one."

Now I really was confused. Who was Aunt May? This whole project was becoming much more complex than I'd anticipated. While I was trying to work out what to say next, Leah woke up. As soon as Grandma heard her cry she leaned forward to look in the stroller and the album slipped from her lap.

We spent the rest of my visit admiring Leah and agreeing that she was quite possibly the most beautiful baby in the world. I didn't feel guilty about this because I knew Grandma said the same thing about each one of her great-grandchildren when she saw them, so as far as I was concerned it was Leah's day of glory.

I kept my promise to the nurse too, and took Leah into the dining room when it was time for Grandma to have her lunch. We walked to the door together, Grandma pushing her walker and me pushing the stroller. Nearly everyone in the care home used walkers or wheelchairs so the corridors were wide. I parked outside the dining room amongst a jumble of walking aids, and lifted Leah out while a caregiver took Grandma's arm and led her to her chair. Then I walked from table to table while Leah stared at everyone around the fingers she had plugged into her mouth. Nobody minded that she didn't smile. Instead they delighted in the softness of her skin and the cushiony plumpness of her legs and arms.

As I watched old fingers reach out to stroke her and listened to the baby talk they had used on their own children decades earlier, I thought of Molly and the baby again. Who were they and why had I never heard of them before?

I was still thinking of them when I reached Grandma's chair and let her give Leah one last kiss. "I'll come again soon," I promised, feeling a bit guilty that my visits were going to be more about Rose than her, and telling myself that it really didn't matter if that was what it took to help her to remember things. It was as I got ready to leave that she surprised me.

"Rose lived in your cottage," she said, her voice clear and the expression on her face entirely lucid.

I swung around, startled. "Rose did?"

She nodded. "When she was a little girl…"

Before she finished the sentence one of the caregivers put a plate of food in front of her, breaking the thread of her thoughts, and within moments she had forgotten that Leah and I had ever been to see her. I turned away, not sure whether to feel frustrated or elated. How long was it going to take me to join all the snippets of her memory together, and when I did, how much more would I have learned about Rose?

* * *

I wanted to tell someone what I'd found out but Ma was out, and despite the fact that none of us had moved far from the village, I didn't have a single sister within walking distance. I wasn't about to confront Millie Carter again either, so calling in at the shop to tell Daniel wasn't an option. With a sigh, I pointed Leah in the direction of home. Then I remembered the notebooks. I had left them on Ma's kitchen table along with the other things I'd found because we had decided not to swamp Gran with memorabilia too soon.

"Time enough if the photos do the trick," Ma had said, stacking the books into a neat pile. She was right of course, but that didn't mean I couldn't read them. Maybe there was stuff in them that would help me talk to Gran about the past. I made a detour to the farm and let myself in through the kitchen door. One thing was for sure, it couldn't do any harm.

Chapter Seven

By the time we arrived home Leah and I were both tired and the sunshine and fresh air had made me ravenous as well. So while Leah napped under the old cherry tree opposite the kitchen door, I made myself a sandwich and took it and an apple out to the porch where I could sit comfortably and still see her. Settling myself in the pock-marked rocking chair that had been there when we moved into the cottage and which was too comfortable to throw away, I opened the first notebook. I nearly choked on my sandwich when I read the words on the flyleaf.

This diary belongs to Rose Petty
Cherry Tree Cottage
Back Lane
Mapleby

IT IS PRIVATE

The words were written in a curly sort of copperplate as if the writer was still deciding how to form perfect letters. I turned to the first page and began to read.

Friday the third of June, 1882:

Today is my twelfth birthday. Mama has made a cake. She has added some CANDIED PEEL to it, and a sprinkle of cinnamon. I have never tasted candied peel but it smells heavenly. I can hardly bear to wait until Papa comes home. When he does we are all going to sit at the table and drink tea and eat cake just like the people do up at the big house. May says I will get above myself but that's because she's jealous. When it was her birthday the hens had stopped laying so there weren't enough eggs for cake and we had to eat bread with some of Mama's best preserve instead.

Tomorrow I will write about the cake. I am going to write something in this diary every single day. <u>It is my best birthday present</u>, better even than the blue ribbon Mama gave me or the old beads May has threaded into a new necklace and which I shall wear to church on Sunday. It was very clever of Papa to know how much I wanted a notebook of my own, one with a proper cover. Writing and drawing on scraps of paper is all very well but stringing them together with wool is not the same. <u>They are not a DIARY.</u>

I turned the page, amused by Rose's enthusiastic use of capitals and underlining, and interested to find out what she thought of the candied peel. As I did so I heard a rumble of distant thunder. It surprised me because the weather had been clear all week and I hadn't seen the slightest wisp of a cloud on my walk. I'm not a country girl for nothing though. I know how quickly a storm can travel, so I slipped Rose's notebook into my pocket, scooped up Leah, who was awake now and watching the leaves blowing in the cherry tree, and hurried indoors. What I saw made me clutch Leah so tightly that she started crying.

Gone were the stripped pine floorboards that I was so proud of, and the dove gray kitchen units. The kitchen table had gone too, and the red and white mugs I kept on the shelf beside the sink. Instead there was a scrubbed deal table with mismatched chairs. Dreary brown linoleum covered the floor, and a black leaded range filled most of one wall. Steam was issuing from the spout of a large copper kettle and the whole room smelled of baking.

Leah stopped crying and her eyes were as round as mine as we watched a pretty dark-haired girl, her hair tied back with a blue ribbon, carefully place a china plate in front of each chair while another, taller girl, whose fair hair was full of honey-coloured streaks, fetched cups and saucers from a cupboard that was built into the space beside the range. So that's what used to be in that alcove, I found myself thinking, and then wondered why I wasn't freaking out and screaming. Maybe it was the sound of the girls' excited chatter, or the cozy warmth of the kitchen that kept me transfixed by the door, or maybe I was rooted to the spot with terror but didn't know it. Whatever it was, it didn't prevent me from listening in.

"I can't believe Mama is letting us use the best china," the dark-haired girl said as she added thin silver knives to the place settings.

"It's because she feels guilty," the tall girl replied, reaching for an old-fashioned tea-caddy and placing it and a brown china teapot at the end of the table nearest to the range.

The smaller girl stopped what she was doing and scowled at her. "Why are you always so mean?"

"I'm not being mean; I'm just telling the truth Rose. You know she didn't want another baby when you were born and you know she feels guilty you found out."

"But I wasn't meant to find out was I, and I wouldn't have if you hadn't told me. Why did you tell me May?"

May's thoughtful expression was tinged with spite as she replied. "I thought you deserved to know the truth."

"Well I didn't want to know the truth and anyway it was a long time ago when Harry and Tom and Daisy were still living at home, and there weren't enough beds, and hardly enough food to go around either. That's what Grandmamma told me anyway."

Another grandmother! I couldn't keep up.

"Well she would wouldn't she? She was trying to make you feel better," May said.

"She wasn't! She just wanted me to understand that it wasn't about me, it was about the situation. How would you like to have another baby when you haven't even got enough money to feed the children you already have?"

"I wouldn't, but it's never going to happen to me because I'm not going to be poor when I grow up."

"But what if you fall in love with a poor person?"

May's pale blue eyes became scornful. "You are so naïve, Rose. That's never going to happen because I intend to marry someone rich. Someone who wants me to use the best china every day, and who will let me employ a maid and a cook so I never need to clean the house or bake my own cakes."

Before Rose could answer a tall figure stepped into the room bringing the smell of horses and leather with him. "So how's the birthday girl?" he said.

Her face full of delight, Rose flung herself at him. "Papa, you came home early."

His eyes twinkled. "It was lucky it was so late in the afternoon when I discovered old Jed needed a new horseshoe, wasn't it?"

She laughed, quick to understand. Then a new and altogether more exciting thought struck her. "Does that mean you've brought him with you?"

"Of course it does and he has a birthday present for you."

Abandoning the table and the dainty china she rushed past him, and somehow I found myself rushing too until we were both in a small orchard where an old carthorse was patiently cropping the grass. He looked up when Rose called his name and a minute later she had flung her arms around him and was resting her cheek against his soft muzzle. When her father joined them her eyes were shining.

"I'm having such a lovely birthday."

"That's because you deserve it, sweetheart," he ruffled the top of her head and there was so much love in his voice that I knew straight away she was his favorite. I wondered if that was what made her sister mean but before I had time to ponder he spoke again.

"Aren't you going to thank Jed for your birthday present then?"

Puzzled, Rose stood back and examined the horse. Then, squealing with excitement, she reached up and plucked two half-open roses from where they were tucked into his harness. The tips of their cream petals were flushed with pink.

"Oh thank you, thank you, thank you, Jed," she kissed the horse's velvety muzzle again and then tucked the flowers into her hair. Her father laughed, and then laughed some more when she paused, hands on hips, and asked for an assurance that he hadn't stolen them.

"Of course I didn't and I can't imagine why you would think so. Anyway, the roses her ladyship grows in the glasshouses are too big and waxy looking for a pretty girl like you. These grew from some prunings someone piled behind the stables years ago."

Satisfied, Rose slipped her hand into his. "Well I love them and I'm going to put them in water when we go indoors so they will last for a long time."

Giving Jed one final pat she began to lead her father back to the cottage. As she did so the door opened and a sturdy woman who was almost completely enveloped in a white apron called to them.

For a moment I thought it was Ma, so great was her resemblance to this woman from another century, then I pulled myself together. Of course it wasn't Ma. She was somewhere in town with my sister Louise…

* * *

"Are you looking for something?" The voice close to my ear brought me back to the here and now with a start, and like smoke blowing in the wind, the scene in front of me dissolved and I found myself standing in the middle of next-door's garden.

I turned towards the man who had asked the question, thinking fast. "Um…I've lost a couple of things from the washing line and I thought they might have blown over the fence."

He shook his head. "I haven't seen anything but I'll bring them round if I find them. You live next door at Cherry Tree Cottage don't you?"

I nodded, then introduced myself, anxious to prove that I wasn't as flaky as I appeared to be. "I'm Rachel. Rachel Ryan, and this is Leah. I'm sorry I didn't ask if I could look around your garden but the house has been empty for so long that I didn't realize there was anyone here."

He smiled. "I'm Robbie Parker, and it's not my garden. I'm just here to do a bit of measuring up for the new owners."

"You're a builder."

"Yes. They've already had their plans approved so I'm just here to work out how much it will all cost."

"It's built on what used to be part of our garden years ago, you know. This was the orchard There were lots of apple trees and there was a huge plum tree right there." I pointed to where Jed had been cropping the grass.

He looked at me in surprise. "How do you know that? This house is at least eighty years old and there's not a single tree in the garden."

Realizing that I was in danger of mixing the past with the present in a way that would do real damage to my credibility I did the only thing I could think of, and said my grandma had told me. Not knowing that I was fast becoming an expert liar, he bought it and changed the subject, asking instead about me and how long I had lived in the cottage. When he discovered I was a village girl born and bred, he quirked an eyebrow.

"Not visited the rest of the world then?"

I shrugged, wishing I wasn't such a sucker for a quirked eyebrow and twinkling blue eyes. "There's still time."

"But not so easy with this one," he touched Leah's cheek, his rough builder's fingers gentle on her silky smooth skin.

"I guess. Anyway, we're kind of rooted here, Daniel and I, because we run the village shop. Well he does at the moment and I used to. I probably will again when Leah is a bit older unless…"

My voice trailed off as a picture of years and years of looking after children began to form itself in my head. In an effort to blot it out, I asked about him. It wasn't my best idea though because by the time he had finished telling me about all the places he'd visited I was green with envy. He was right. I needed to see what life was like outside Mapleby. Perhaps Daniel and I could rent out the shop and the cottage and go somewhere else for a while, before we had any more children. Even as I thought it, I knew it wasn't going to happen, not yet anyway and probably not ever, because I was still Rachel, the Pavelak girl who'd had some sort of breakdown. Rachel who needed to stay near her family just in case it happened again.

Remembering that brought me squarely back to the here and now and why I was in the middle of next door's garden. Had I really seen Rose and her sister? Had her father really tethered a newly shod carthorse to lowest branch of a plum tree that was no longer here, or had I dreamt it all? I needed time to think about it...alone...before Daniel came home. With little more than a perfunctory farewell I pushed open the gate and made my way back to the cottage. If Robbie Parker watched me go, I didn't notice. I heard him though, and when he called out that we would be seeing a lot more of one another as soon as the building started, I decided to ignore the little flip I felt in my stomach.

Chapter Eight

By the time Daniel arrived home I was sure I had imagined everything. I even told him about it in a roundabout way, saying I'd fallen asleep while I was reading Rose's diary and dreamt about what she had written. He pretended to be interested but I knew he wasn't really, although he did want to know about my visit to Grandma. When I told him how much she enjoyed watching the birds he looked pleased, and he looked even more pleased when I kissed him and told him he was the best grandson-in-law she had.

I left him and Leah together while I finished cooking the evening meal, and as soon as he had tucked her into her crib I poured him a glass of wine and then stood sipping tonic water as I waited for the vegetables to finish cooking. We smiled at one another, the problems of the past forgiven if not quite forgotten, and I told him about Robbie Parker. Well not about Robbie but about how the house next door had been sold and how the new owners had employed a builder to give it a makeover before they moved in.

He was interested in that because he has an eye for design and enjoys making things. In another life I think he would have liked to be an architect but there you go, we can't have everything we want, and he always seems happy enough pottering about making improvements to the cottage and the shop. Anyway, we talked about the house next door for a while, then we ate our meal, and finally, in the space between washing up and Leah waking for her evening feed, we found the time and the energy to make love.

It wasn't spectacular because neither of us were turned on in the way we had been earlier in the week, but it was okay, and afterwards we lay in one another's arms talking about what we were going to do the following day. It was then that I remembered his trip to town and asked him about it.

He rolled over on his back and stared at the ceiling. "Everything was fine, and afterwards I went to see Millie's grandfather."

I was completely nonplussed. "Whatever for?"

"He put an interesting proposition to me a couple of days ago. At the time I told him I'd think about it and get back to him."

"So you were getting back to him. Don't beat about the bush, Daniel. What does he want?"

"He wants me…us, to consider renting out the rooms over the shop."

I twisted my neck so I could look at him, but in the shadow of the evening I couldn't read the expression on his face. I frowned. "Why? Does he run some sort of business or…," I knew the answer before I finished the question? "He wants it for Millie, doesn't he? Millie and her children?"

He moved his head on the pillow in a way that I interpreted as a yes as he replied. "She's been given a month's notice by the landlord of the place where she is now, and she's struggling to find anything else suitable in Mapleby."

"So he thinks our storerooms might be the answer, does he? I suppose Millie put him up to it."

"Probably, but I don't blame her. Ever since her husband bailed out she and her children been living in one grubby bedsit after another, so of course she wants to move into the space above the shop. It's clean and it has a decent kitchen and a bathroom…"

"I know what it has, Daniel. I also know that it's where we store a lot of our stock. It's where we make coffee and eat our lunch too. It's even where we go when we need to use the bathroom for goodness sake, so how is that going to work if Millie moves in?"

Before he could answer, Leah began to stir. With a frustrated sigh, I swung my feet out of bed and pulled on my old silk dressing gown, the one that showed up every one of my curves and which had a habit of slipping undone at the most inopportune moments. It was, if the truth were known, at least partly responsible for Leah's conception.

Instead of watching, like he always did when I shrugged myself into it, he kept his eyes firmly fixed on the ceiling, and that was when I knew he had already agreed. Maybe not in writing and he probably hadn't set a date or anything, he had just been waiting for the right time to tell me. To say I was angry was an understatement but with Leah beginning to cry in earnest, now was not the time to discuss it.

"We'll talk about this later," I told him. Then I hurried through to the nursery. By the time I returned to the bedroom Daniel was fast asleep, one long leg outside the covers and his arms thrown wide across the bed. For a moment I contemplated waking him and having an argument right then and there, but I didn't. Instead I slipped into bed beside him and thought about the implications of Millie Carter living above the shop. Then I thought about Rose and how my imagination had got the better of me earlier that day. Then, just as I was dropping off to sleep, I thought about the twinkle in Robbie Parker's blue eyes.

* * *

Leah was fractious the following morning, and Daniel was late, so any discussion about Millie Carter had to wait. To work off my anger, I cleaned the cottage from top to bottom, emptied the ironing basket and then, in an excess of energy, decided to weed the front path. Leah, who once she had recovered from her earlier irritability had gurgled and chuckled her way around the cottage as I lugged her from room to room, was tired out, so I parked the stroller under the cherry tree and left her sleeping.

I'd almost reached the end of the path when the gate clicked and I found myself looking up at Robbie Parker. He was wearing a t-shirt and jeans the same as yesterday, and his hair was just as tousled. This time though, I noticed it was so dark it was almost blue black. His eyes were also bluer than I remembered. He smiled a sexy, lop-sided grin.

"Hello again."

I straightened up. "Hello."

"I...uh...I've come to beg for a glass of water. Next door's water is still turned off at the mains and I'm parched after spending the past hour digging down to look at the damp course."

I pointed to the rocking chair. "I can do better than that if you can wait until I've washed my hands."

I knew, when I returned with the beer and wearing a fresh slick of lip-gloss, that I was being provocative, but I didn't care. If Daniel was going to spend half his life worrying about Millie Carter instead of spending time with Leah and me, then I wasn't going to feel guilty.

Popping the can open, Robbie tilted it to his lips and took a long drink. Watching him, I noticed what I had missed in the confusion of our first meeting, that as well as being tall, he was tanned and muscled and looked very fit. I turned away as soon as he lowered the can but I knew he had seen me staring.

"Do you want me to open one for you?" He gestured to where I had dropped a four-pack of beer onto the grass beside him.

I nodded. One weak beer wasn't going to harm Leah, not now she was down to three breast feeds a day. When he handed me the can our fingers touched. The unexpected contact sent a sharp surge of lust through me, as unexpected as it was disturbing. Muttering that I just needed to check on Leah I hurried across the garden, beer sloshing onto my shaking fingers. What the hell was I doing?

Looking at the crescents of Leah's long, dark eyelashes curving across her cheek brought me to my senses. So what if my quest for a little fun had turned out to be a bit more than I expected, no-one would ever know. Robbie Parker probably hadn't even noticed the effect he had on me. I walked slowly back towards him, settled on the grass and asked him what was happening next door.

"Building is starting in two weeks," he said. Then he nodded towards Leah's pram. "While we're knocking walls down it might be too noisy for her to sleep outdoors."

I stared at him. "I thought you were renovating it for the new owners, not demolishing it."

"I am, but as they want it open plan there's quite a bit of bashing about to do."

"Is bashing about a builder's technical term?" I asked with a grin, feeling a lot more relaxed now we were talking about other people.

He laughed. "I can show you the plans if you like. They're pinned to the wall in the kitchen."

Nosiness fought with caution and won out, and a couple of minutes later I was pushing a still sleeping Leah through next door's gate and round to the back of the house. Robbie walked ahead, clearing a spade and a pickaxe out of the way for me. Leaving Leah beside the kitchen door, I went inside.

Despite the hot weather, it felt cold and damp. I shivered slightly. "It's very dark."

He nodded, serious now we were looking at the plans. "That's why the new owners want it opened out. We're going to take out the wall overlooking the garden and put in a long run of bi-fold doors."

I shook my head. "You've lost me already. What are bi-fold doors?"

"They're just fancy patio doors that open right up. In the winter the room will be warm but it will still be bright and airy because the whole wall will be glass. In the summer the doors can be folded right back so the room is completely open to the garden."

I listened as he explained the finer points of the architect's drawing pinned to the wall in front of me. It sounded as if whoever was buying the house had a lot of money to spare. I asked if he knew them. He shook his head.

"I haven't met them but I know they're American. I think they're moving to the UK because of his job.

"Why Mapleby though?"

He chuckled. "Why not?"

"Well, for a start it's in the back of beyond. There's not much going on here, is there? I can't imagine it's got anything that would attract foreigners, especially Americans. Don't they insist on walk-in fridges and huge washing machines and stuff?"

He was really laughing at me now. "Maybe they're not those sort of Americans, and even if they are it doesn't make them bad people."

I shook my head. "I'm just jealous of the bi-fold doors."

"You can have them too. They're easy enough to install."

"Everything is easy if you have money," I said gloomily. Then I brightened up. "Perhaps one of their ancestors came from Mapleby and they are going to research their family tree. Americans are always interested in their past aren't they?"

"I wouldn't know because I don't have any American friends and I don't think you have either. I don't think you've even met an American, what with living in all your life in this boring little backwater."

Although I laughed at his teasing I knew he was right. Mapleby was the sort of place that only attracted hikers and dog owners, those hearty outdoor types who were happy with pub grub and a pint of beer. Exotic it was not, although the countryside surrounding it was very beautiful.

I was about to answer with a piece of face-saving repartee when, always anxious about Leah, I glanced out of the open doorway to check on her, and saw Rose. She was sitting on a swing that had been fixed to the upper branches of the old plum tree at the bottom of the garden, and her face had a dreamy look as she swung gently to and fro. Even as I saw her I remembered there were no longer any trees in the garden and the confusion must have showed in my face.

"Are you okay Rachel? You look as if you've just seen a ghost." There was concern in Robbie's voice as he moved across to the door and peered through it. I knew he wouldn't be able to see Rose, or the tree, or the swing. I knew too that what he had just said was true. I had seen a ghost. What I didn't understand was why it was this version of Rose, not the one who sometimes stood beside Leah's crib in the mornings. At the same time that these thoughts flashed through my mind I was searching for a way to explain my odd behavior.

"I'm fine. I thought I saw someone in the garden but it was just a shadow, probably a dark cloud drifting in front of the sun or something." I turned to leave.

Taking his cue from me, Robbie nodded and then followed me out of the house, locking the door behind us. I made my excuses, saying Leah needed feeding. Then I thanked him for showing me the plans and carried on chattering inanely, anxious to deflect his attention from the sky. So much for my excuse about a cloud. There wasn't even a wisp of white, just a great arched dome of forget-me-not blue, the same color as the ribbon Rose had been wearing in her hair.

He pushed the pram back down to the path for me and maneuvered it through the gate. Leah was awake now and she gave him a toothless grin when he spoke to her. "You tell your mother to stop jumping at shadows young lady. Tell her it's time she got out more."

I was sure his words were laced with double meaning. Even though he wasn't going to pursue it, he didn't for a moment believe my excuse about the clouds. He didn't think much of my way of life either, so if I was up for it, he was going to stir things up a bit. The thought was enough to send me hotfoot back to the safety of my own cottage with barely a backward glance.

He watched me go, his eyes full of a sardonic humor which I tried hard to ignore. Robbie Parker could see right through me in a way that made me squirm. He knew I had some sort of secret, he knew I was fed up with the sameness of my life and, worse, he knew I found him far too attractive for my own good, and I had a feeling he intended to play it every which way he knew.

I concentrated on Leah for the rest of the afternoon, ignoring the sporadic hammering noises coming from next door and the fact that Robbie Parker's van was still on the grass verge. I didn't venture anywhere near the garden until I heard him start up the engine, and even then I waited until I was sure he had disappeared over the brow of the hill before I popped Leah into her baby carrier, strapped it to my chest, and went next door again.

It had been empty since long before we moved into the cottage but I had never trespassed before. Now though, I had no qualms. Whoever had inherited it from the original owner who had died years ago, had obviously sold it to some nameless Americans who weren't about to visit any time soon, so I could explore the garden as much as I pleased.

Although it was quite late in the afternoon, the sky was still cloudless and blue as I pushed open the gate and retraced my steps down the garden path and then beyond, to the very end of the garden where I had seen Rose sitting on the swing. It wasn't there of course, and nor was the tree. In their place was a flower bed full of weeds, a pile of broken flower pots and an upended wheelbarrow. I leaned against the wheelbarrow and look around. Robbie was right. There wasn't a tree in sight. Nothing at all to suggest that it had once been an orchard.

I had come prepared though. I pulled a small notepad out of my pocket and quickly sketched the shape of the garden onto a blank page. Then, screwing up my eyes, I concentrated on recalling exactly where I had seen the trees. I couldn't remember all of them but I managed almost a dozen, including the plum tree where I'd seen Jed grazing and then seen Rose on her swing. When I finished I studied the result and quickly realized that the orchard had been cleared to make room for the house because half the trees were slap bang in the middle of the plot. For a moment it made me sad, then a thought struck me. If the orchard had once been part of my cottage's garden, who had sold off the land, and why? Was it Rose's parents, or even Rose herself after they died? I would probably never know. It was intriguing though because even in Mapleby where we had more trees than you could shake a stick at, cutting them down was frowned upon. It took months of form filling, telephone calls, and a visit from a purse-lipped councilor before a tree could be felled, even if its roots were undermining a house. I know because it had happened to Daniel and me when we first bought the cottage, and the bureaucracy had filled me with fury. Then I shook my head. Rules and regulations were probably totally different nowadays. I had to stop imposing my twenty-first century thoughts onto life in the nineteenth century.

Although Leah loved being in her carrier, she was beginning to get restless. I knew it was her teatime but I wanted to walk right around the garden before I went home. Soothed by the silly songs I sang as I clambered around to the side of the house that was hidden from the road, she started smiling again. I was midway through my third tuneless rendering of her favorite nursery rhyme when I froze mid-tune because there, nailed to a rickety old fence, was a horseshoe. It wasn't any old horseshoe either. It was huge, the sort of shoe a carthorse would wear. Carefully, I stepped over the debris of old furniture and broken planks that must have been there for years, and stood in front of the fence.

The horseshoe had obviously been there for a very long time because it was encrusted with grime and there was the beginning of a strange yellow growth on parts of it. I put up my hand to brush the worst of it away and as I did so I saw the words etched into the space inside the arch of the horseshoe.

Jed

Died 10 July 1884

And underneath, very small, was the shape of a heart.

From the look of it, someone had used a hot poker to burn the words into the wooden plank of the fence, and I knew it was Rose because her father wouldn't have drawn a heart, although he might have hammered the horseshoe onto the fence for her.

I took a photo with my cell phone. Here was something else to show Grandma. Maybe she would be able to remember something about the cottage and the orchard if I prompted her.

Chapter Nine

While I was feeding Leah her tea, Daniel phoned to say he would be late. I didn't ask why. Instead I built up a steam of resentment as I bathed her and got her ready for bed. It was Millie Carter again. I was sure of it. He was probably helping her decide where her furniture was going in the rooms over our shop, or repairing the dripping tap in the kitchen that I had been telling him to mend for ages, or maybe he was meeting her grandfather again and signing a rental agreement without discussing it with me.

By the time Leah was asleep I felt so sorry for myself that I couldn't be bothered to cook. Instead I made myself a cheese sandwich and decided Daniel could have the same when he came home. Then, ignoring the unwashed dishes in the kitchen, I took Rose's diary out of the drawer where I'd put the pile of notebooks for safe keeping, and settled down to read it.

If I expected to be sucked into a time warp again then I was disappointed because nothing untoward happened as I devoured her daily entries. By several pages in, however, I had built up a picture of a fairly leisurely life. It really surprised me because Ma is forever telling me and all my sisters how lucky we are compared to when she was young. Grandma used to do the same before she began to forget things, so I thought I knew all there was to know about the hardships of rural life in the past. Rose's description of her life was so different, however, that it took me a while to realize she got off lightly because she was the baby of the family.

From the diary entries it was obvious that May worked harder, although not very willingly, and who could blame her when her little sister spent all her time outside in the sunshine while she had to help her mother in the house. The other sister, Daisy, was rarely mentioned at all because she was a maid at a house several miles away, and Rose hardly ever saw her. Her brothers, Harry and Joseph, were away too. Harry was a farm laborer, married with a child of his own, and Joseph was a junior footman somewhere in London. The only time Rose mentioned him was when he wrote home to say he had just been promoted. She wasn't very complimentary about it either, saying his ambition to be a butler seemed a very dull thing to her.

By the time her entries became more sporadic, I had gone off her a little bit because she didn't appear to care about anybody's feelings except her own. Then I remembered how young she was, and how every teenager was fixated on their own world, and I forgave her. I wasn't so sure about her parents though. Couldn't they see they were storing up trouble for her by letting her skip chores and be forgetful? The thought that maybe I had been brought up the same way didn't enter my head then, or for many weeks afterwards.

The sound of Daniel's van interrupted my thoughts and suddenly I wanted to talk to him about Rose's diary, so I decided not to be angry with him any more. Instead of the cheese sandwich I had planned, I would cook him his favorite ham and cheese omelet with all the trimmings. I was halfway through slitting open a bag of oven ready fries when he came into the kitchen and dumped a couple of plastic bags on the table. One of them toppled over, spilling a couple of overripe bananas.

"I thought you could make some banana bread with those," he said, tipping the rest of the contents of the bag into the fruit bowl.

I bit my lip because I hated having to use up things he hadn't managed to sell. I wasn't going to lose my temper though. Besides, Grandma enjoyed banana bread and I was planning to visit her again the following day. I let the milk that had reached its use-by-date go too, and the packs of cold meat.

"You must have read my mind," I said brightly, tearing open one of the packets and beginning to chop the ham.

He walked around the table to where I was standing and hugged me because he knew how I felt. "I'm sorry, Rachel, I over-ordered for the deli counter and then forgot to tell Millie to discount it."

I wanted to say surely she could have worked it out for herself but I stopped myself, partly because I knew she hadn't been working there for long enough to understand how carefully we had to manage the stock, and partly because I didn't want her to start making the decisions I used to make on a daily basis when I was working. Once she did that my fate was doomed. First he would say she was doing well, then he would say she was indispensable and surely I'd rather stay at home with Leah all day until she started school and I wasn't sure I wanted to do that, so I never uttered a word. Instead, I laid a place at the table, poured him a beer, and told him to sit down.

He did so gratefully and it was then that I noticed how tired he looked. Immediately I felt guilty. Was I responsible for the shadows under his eyes and that new hollowing beneath his cheeks? He saw the question on my face and gave a weary smile.

"It's just work, Rach. We were getting a bit low on some things so I had to make an extra trip to the wholesalers today, and by the time I got back school was out so I had to serve in the shop instead of unloading the car."

He knew, as soon as he said it, that he had dropped himself in it, and this time I couldn't keep the sarcasm out of my voice. "The result of employing Millie Carter, I suppose. Anyone else could have stayed to help but she had to collect her boys from school, didn't she? I can't imagine what you were thinking of, taking her on. I suppose you had to do all the lifting on your own as well."

In the past Pa used to help with the heavy things, even going to the wholesaler for us sometimes, but he wouldn't any more, not since he injured his back lifting a heavy pack of forty-eight shrink-wrapped tins from the trunk of the car. I was about to mention this when Daniel shook his head.

"That's where you're wrong because Millie came back after she collected the boys and they all helped, even the

75

little one, although his main aim seemed to be to carry in the sweets." He smiled as he said it and although I tried to ignore it, I suddenly had a mental picture of a cozy togetherness: Daniel carting in the heavy stuff while Millie re-stocked the shelves and the little boys dragged in a few of the smaller boxes. A sudden surge of jealousy made me spiteful.

"So now you're paying her overtime as well I suppose, and you'll have given the boys some sweets, too. It's got to stop Daniel, because we can't afford to sub Millie Carter, however sorry you feel for her."

He took a long drink before he answered but when he did I knew I had overstepped the mark. "As it happens, Millie wouldn't take a penny extra. She came back because she said it was her fault we were low on some things, so the least she could do was help to put it right. She wouldn't let me give the little boys sweets either. She said they had to learn to help out without expecting a reward every time they did something."

"So she's buttering you up until you've made a decision about the rooms above the shop."

He shook his head. "No Rachel, she was just being helpful, the same as you were before you discovered you had a sharp tongue."

I turned away and concentrated on grating the cheese because I didn't want to see the disappointment in his eyes. I didn't apologize though. Instead I asked him when we were going to talk about it.

"Whenever you like," he said, and his voice hardened as he got up and poured himself another beer.

I swung round and scowled at him. "You've already decided, haven't you? And you've told Millie."

He nodded. "It's a no brainer because Millie's grandfather has offered to pay for the decorating and repairs and he's going to help Millie with the rent too, so what is there to discuss? We can't afford to turn down such a good offer and you know it. Besides, having someone living over the premises makes the shop far more secure.

With Millie there I won't get those middle of the night calls when some night creature triggers the security alarm."

I knew he had me and if it had been anyone other than Millie Carter I would have been thrilled. Renting out the rooms above the shop was not only going to help offset the fact that we now only had one wage coming in, they would be decorated as well, something we had been meaning to get around to ever since we took it over.

I finished cooking the omelet and tipped it and the fries onto a plate. Sliding it across the table I gave him a sheepish smile. "You're right. I guess being here on my own all day makes me a bit irrational at times. It's a good decision and I'm sure Millie appreciates it."

He nodded and then tucked into his meal and we didn't mention it again. I didn't say a word about what I had been doing that day though because somewhere in the middle of our argument about Millie Carter, I lost my wish to share. If he was going to make arbitrary decisions, then I was going to keep everything I had learned about Rose to myself. I wasn't going to tell him anything about the house next door or Robbie Parker either.

* * *

The next day Ma was already at the nursing home when I arrived with Leah and the freshly baked banana bread, and she greeted me with a relieved smile. "You must have a sixth sense or something, Grandma has been talking about you ever since I arrived, not that I've been able to make head nor tail of what she's on about."

I lifted Leah out of the pram and plumped her down on her great-grandmother's ample lap. "Hello Grandma, how are you today?"

She gave me a sharp look. "You've made Rose sad."

Ma rolled her eyes.

Wondering how best to deal with the effect the photos had obviously had on Grandma's tenuous hold on reality, I sank into the chair opposite her and leaned forward. "What have I done?"

"Blue eyes aren't everything." Her voice dripped with disappointment.

Although it sounded like nonsense I knew straight away she was talking about Robbie Parker and an involuntary shiver ran up my spine. Ma snorted.

"I'm going to fetch her a cup of tea. It'll give her something else to focus on," she said in a muffled whisper.

I waited until she'd gone before I answered my grandmother. "Why did me talking to Robbie make Rose sad?"

"Because she did it too." For a brief moment Gran's eyes were full of lucidity but then she retreated into confusion, and by the time Ma returned with a tray of tea for all of us, she was asking me who Leah's parents were.

* * *

For the next half-hour we chatted about inconsequential things while we all watched Leah as she rolled around on the blanket I'd spread out on the carpet. I didn't forget though, and when I was sure I could be trusted to keep my voice casual, I scrolled through the photos on my cell phone. The picture of the horseshoe and the writing beneath it was very clear. I held it out to Grandma.

"Did Rose do this?"

Ma frowned. "Don't encourage her, Rachel," she muttered. I ignored her.

Grandma peered at the photo. "Jed died," she said.

"I know he did. Do you know what happened?"

She nodded and her voice became dreamy as she recalled something she had been told in the dim and distant past of her childhood. "Granny Rose said he was pulling the cart and it was heavy, and he fell down and he was dead."

"Did she see it happen?"

"Rose was on the cart. She should have been in the kitchen but she was on the cart."

Thanks to those diary entries, I could see it all. Instead of helping her mother, Rose had slipped away under the pretext of taking a message to her father at the big house, and he, always happy to indulge her, had pulled her up onto the cart and given her a ride. It had been while they were laughing together that poor Jed, already old and probably overworked, had a heart attack. He died still harnessed to the cart he had pulled for the whole of his life.

"She couldn't bear it. She cried for days and days and made herself ill. She didn't stop until her Papa brought home the horseshoe and nailed it to the fence."

Ma plucked the phone out of Grandma's hand while she was still talking. After staring at the picture for a moment, she looked at me in confusion. "Well at least you seem to know what's she's talking about."

I gave her a half smile. "Not really, although I'm beginning to piece things together. Apparently Granny Rose lived in our cottage when she was a little girl. In those days the garden was much bigger and there was an orchard. It was where the house next door is now. Granny Rose's Father worked with horses up at the big house, wherever that was, and Jed, the horse who this shoe belonged to, was Rose's favorite, so he sometimes brought him home and tethered him in the orchard under the plum tree."

"And you've found all this out from those old notebooks?"

"Yes," I lied. Then, to put myself in the clear in case anyone else decided to read them. "Well, those and listening to Grandma. She can remember quite a lot when she's in the mood."

"Hmm, so there is something in this suggestion that we keep talking to her about the past, is there?"

"It seems so," I nodded. Then Leah began to cry because she had managed to wedge herself into a gap between two chairs. By the time I'd extricated her and smothered her with kisses until she was laughing again, it was time for Grandma's tea, so I didn't have to say anything else.

* * *

I walked back to the farm with Ma, listening with pretended fascination while she recounted her day in town with Louise. By the time we got there Leah was hungry so I fed her sitting in the sun on the back porch while Ma watered the tubs of geraniums. I had almost finished when she came and sat beside me.

"There was a scandal of some sort you know…about Granny Rose," she said.

I stared at her. "What do you mean, a scandal?"

She shrugged. "She had some sort of nervous breakdown I think, although I've no idea why. I probably heard about it when I was listening where I shouldn't have been. Maybe Grandma will be able to tell you on one of her good days."

"You must know more than that," I said hurriedly because I didn't want her to suddenly remember I'd had some sort of breakdown too and try to change the subject.

She shook her head. "People didn't talk about things openly in those days, they just whispered in corners, but when I was a very small I discovered that if I sat, quiet as a mouse under the kitchen table, I could learn their secrets. It had a green baize cloth that used to hang almost to the floor so no one knew I was there."

I grinned at her, remembering how I used to hide behind the sofa listening to my sisters. It was where I'd learned the facts of life and a whole lot of other useful things, and it was how I had gleaned enough secrets to be able to embarrass them whenever their boyfriends came to call. Ma saw the thought and laughed

"You too, Rachel. It's what happens when you're the youngest because it's the only way you can find out anything at all."

* * *

I remembered what Ma had said later that evening when I settled down to read some more of Rose's diary. It was slow work because after the enthusiasm of the first few carefully written pages her handwriting became far more difficult to decipher as she experimented with different styles in the way of all teenagers. Sometimes the writing was so small I had to screw up my eyes to make sense of it. I ploughed on though, because I was sure she would have written something about Jed.

I found the entry halfway through the notebook. I knew it was the right place before I even started reading because she had edged the whole page with black ink. To say she was devastated was an understatement. The writing was blurred in places, presumably from her tears. I didn't learn anything new though, not on that page. The next one, however, opened up a whole lot of possibilities, and this time it was about May.

Today Mama and Papa gave in and said May can go and work in the village. She has been pleading and crying about it for months and now they have agreed. She is going to work for Miss Acton. As soon as they told her she could go she stopped being mean and lent me her best black ribbon for my hair so everyone can see how sad I am about dear old Jed.

I cannot imagine why she wants to work for Miss Acton, who is tall and thin and never smiles, but she does. May even asked if she can live in the village during the week, but Papa said no. He says she has to come home every evening, even in the winter. She got those two red spots on her cheeks that she always gets when she's angry, but she didn't say a word. She will ask again though, I'm sure of it. Once she has been working for a while she will find a way of persuading Mama and Papa to let her stay with Aunt Mabel during the week and then I will have the bedroom all to myself. What bliss!

I leaned back in the chair with the notebook open on my lap and stared into space. Did teenage girls really work in shops all those years ago when Rose was young? I supposed they must have. I wished I had concentrated more in my history lessons at school.

Daniel, who was trying to balance the week's takings, looked across at me from where he was sitting at the table. "You look serious."

I smiled at him. Things had been good between us this evening. He had come home early and played with Leah before I put her to bed and then, while I was settling her, had heated up a lasagna he had brought home from our specials counter and opened a bottle of wine. He hadn't mentioned Millie Carter once either, so with no reason to stoke up the feeling of resentment I'd been nurturing all week, I told him about Rose's diaries. He was more interested than I expected him to be, and we spent the rest of the evening looking at various history sites on the Internet as we tried to buff up our knowledge of the past.

Chapter Ten

When I woke up the following morning Daniel wasn't lying in bed beside me like he usually did on a Sunday. I could hear him moving about in the kitchen and I stretched luxuriously, sure that he was treating me to breakfast in bed. He had obviously realized how unfair it was to abandon Leah and me each morning just so Millie Carter could get her children to school, and this was his way of saying sorry. Deciding to be gracious about it, I plumped up the pillows and waited.

I was still waiting when I heard Leah stir. I let her whimper for a minute or two, so sure was I that Daniel would fetch her, but when she started crying in earnest I threw back the bedcovers and went into the nursery. Rose was already there, leaning over the cot, although she backed off when she saw me. I scowled at her.

"Stop telling tales."

Her beautiful dark eyes widened into a question. "You told Grandma about Robbie Parker," I said, completely unfazed by the fact that I was arguing with a ghost, although admittedly it takes two to argue and, true to form, Rose wasn't saying anything. Briefly I wondered why I could hear her speak when I slipped through whatever time warp it was that took me back to her childhood, but not in the here and now, then I shook my head.

"None of it is true...well not in the way you seem to think. It's not like it was when you were my age. In the twenty-first century it's possible to be friends with someone of the opposite sex without it meaning a thing, and that's what Robbie is, he's just a friend. Actually he's not even a friend really, he's just someone who is going to be working next door for a while, so I can hardly ignore him, can I?"

To my amazement her eyes filled with tears. Even though she had started it all, it still made me feel a bit mean. I tried again. "Look, I don't know how you manage to talk to Grandma when the rest of us have trouble getting her to understand a single word we say, but I'd rather you didn't. She is confused enough as it is. I'd rather you stopped dropping in on Leah too…"

I was still talking to her when Daniel came into the nursery. He grinned at me. "That sounded a bit of a deep conversation you were having with Leah. I know you don't believe in baby talk but she's probably a bit young to share the family's angst over your grandmother."

Wondering exactly what he had heard I watched him lift Leah out of the cot and saw the delight on her face as he jiggled her up and down. "I was talking to myself really," I said, and because Rose had disappeared the moment Daniel entered the room, I wondered if that was closer to the truth than I cared to admit.

Maybe I was still suffering from the after effects of the anti-depressants I had taken after Leah was born, pills that had over-stimulated my imagination. If I had never seen Rose's photo or read her diary I probably wouldn't be staring at the space where she'd been standing a few moments before, wondering where she had gone. It would explain why Daniel and Ma couldn't see her, either. It didn't explain Leah though. Leah had stopped crying and was smiling up at Rose when I walked into the nursery, and Rose was smiling back at her. Surely I hadn't imagined that as well. There was Grandma too. Even Ma had heard what she said although she had dismissed it as confused nonsense. I shook my head to clear my thoughts.

Daniel saw me and frowned. "Are you okay, Rach?"

I forced a smile. "Never better. What are we having for breakfast?"

He looked shamefaced. "Um…I need to talk to you about that."

I knew what he was going to say, so I said it for him. "I know, you've got to go and see Millie Carter's grandfather because he wants to talk about paint colors or something equally important."

"Don't be like that. He rang yesterday to say could I show a builder around to get an idea of costs. I'll only be an hour or so."

"But why Sunday? It's the only day we have together, Daniel. Didn't you think of that when you agreed?"

"I know I should have, but this builder guy is doing it on the cheap as some sort of favor. Apparently he has a big building contract somewhere else in the village which keeps him busy during the day but he's offered to work at the shop in the evening and at weekends."

A dim light bulb flickered in the back of my brain. "Have you met him?"

He shook his head as he hoisted Leah into a more comfortable position. "Not yet and I've just had a very good idea. Why don't you come too? We can skip breakfast for brunch at the pub instead."

"What about Leah?"

"I'll spoon baby rice into her while you get ready, and then you can breastfeed her while I load all her paraphernalia into the van."

For a moment I was tempted to throw his offer back in his face, so disappointed was I that, far from preparing a surprise breakfast, he had been making arrangements to go out. I didn't though because I didn't feel inclined to cut off my nose to spite my face. Besides, if this mystery builder turned out to be Robbie Parker, then an official introduction would be a good idea. Maybe I could choose some of the paint colors too. After all, it was our shop, Daniel's and mine. Millie Carter would just be living there.

* * *

When we met him outside the shop, Robbie took my hand in his large one and gave me a slow smile.

85

"Rachel and I have already met. Leah too." He turned to Daniel. "And I'm afraid I drank one of your cans of beer on that very hot day last week."

Seeing the wicked twinkle in his eye I realized he had no intention of explaining himself further so I dived in, babbling more than necessary.

"Robbie is working on the house next door to ours," I said. "You remember I told you about it, how the new owners are American and they are having the whole thing gutted and refitted before they move in."

I wasn't at all sure I'd told him any such thing and I knew, from the expression on his face, that he was doubtful too. He wasn't about to say so in company though, so he merely nodded, smiled, and shook Robbie's hand.

"I guess that means we'll be seeing quite a lot of you over the next few weeks, what with you working next door as well as renovating the rooms over the shop."

* * *

An hour later, I found myself sitting next to Daniel and opposite Robbie while we waited for our Sunday brunch to arrive. Leah was sleeping peacefully in her pram beside us. I had no idea whether Robbie had invited himself or if it was Daniel who had suggested it, but I felt very uncomfortable.

I was the only one who did, though. The men were already bonding over football as they picked apart the results of the season's matches and tried to forecast what would happen next year. Neither of them appeared to take any notice of me when I left them to it and went over to the bar to see Tom.

"Any news from Ella?" I asked a bit too brightly because I had just caught sight of Robbie Parker's reflection in the mirror behind the bar and I could see he was watching me.

"Yes, she's somewhere in the Caribbean until the end of the month, then it's back to London for a week or so before she flies to Paris."

"You sound like her diary secretary," I teased, and then wished I hadn't been so flippant when I saw the misery in his eyes.

He shrugged. "That's what it feels like, Rachel. She's very good at keeping me up to date with her travel plans. I can't fault her for that. I just wish her phone calls and emails were a bit more personal. She never tells me anything about what her life is like when she's not working. Does she ever talk to you about it?"

I shook my head, wishing I could say yes. "She doesn't really talk to me at all Tom, not since I had Leah. I guess we don't have much in common now I'm a stay-at-home mum."

He sighed as he filled a glass with orange juice and pushed it across the bar towards me. "Here, have that on the house. If I can't feed Ella at least I can look after you."

I thanked him and then, taking a sip, asked a question that had been on my mind for quite a while. "You don't think there's anything wrong, do you?"

He stared at me and I could see the panic starting to build. "In what way?"

I shrugged it off. "Don't mind me. Since I had Leah I worry about everything. It drives Daniel mad. I'm sure Ella is fine. Busy, but fine."

He gave a reluctant nod. "You're probably right. I'm just glad her mother isn't here to see how she's changed because if she was it would break her heart. Between you and me I think it was Ella who kept her going for so long. She was so brave when Ella went to London, waving her off with such a big smile so no one would know her heart was breaking."

Remembering how quickly his wife had succumbed to the cancer that had stalked her for years once Ella left Mapleby, I patted his hand. "She was very proud of Ella, wasn't she?"

He gripped my fingers and I was surprised to see how knotted with arthritis they were. To me Tom had always been a big, burly rugby player, someone whose natural place was behind a bar once he could no longer run as fast or score the tries that had made him a local hero when I was little. When had he started to get so old?

"You're right. She was very proud, but she would have been just as proud if Ella had decided to stay in Mapleby and settle down like you and Daniel."

As I walked back to the table I pondered his remark. Ella had never talked about settling down and having children. Instead she had played the field, laughing at me because I only wanted Daniel.

"I can't believe you're going to marry the village shopkeeper," she said, the night I told her we were getting engaged. She liked Daniel well enough, even admitted that as local catches went he was up there with the best, but I had always known I'd disappointed her. Meeting Robbie's eyes and seeing the shadow of a question in them, I crossed my fingers as I slid into my seat. I hoped I wasn't going to be disappointed that I had chosen Daniel too.

Nobody said anything until the waitress had placed plates piled high with bacon, eggs, tomatoes and hash browns in front of us, then Daniel raised an eyebrow. "How is Tom?"

I shrugged. "The same as usual."

"He hasn't heard from Ella then."

"It's not that. He says he hears from her all the time, it's just that she never really tells him anything."

Robbie squeezed a sachet of brown sauce onto his plate and looked interested. Daniel explained. "Tom's daughter, Ella, is a make-up artist who spends most of her life working on various film sets around the world."

"It sounds exotic."

"I guess it is but it doesn't suit Tom. His wife died shortly after Ella moved to London so now all he has is the pub, and he's lonely."

"Doesn't she ever come home?"

"Not often. It upsets you as well, doesn't it, Rachel? Rachel and Ella were almost inseparable when they were growing up. Without Ella's approval I don't think I would have stood a chance!"

I laughed as I tried to make light of it because I didn't feel comfortable talking about Ella to a stranger. I searched for a way to change the subject without being rude. "Don't take any notice of Daniel. He likes to exaggerate. I was only friendly with her because she had a bedroom of her own while my house was so full of Pavalaks that I never had more than five minute's privacy at any time."

"Pavalaks?"

"My maiden name."

"So you're Rachel Pavalak."

A curious inflection in his voice made me respond more sharply than I intended. "I was Rachel Pavalak. Now I'm Rachel Ryan."

He smiled. "Sorry. It's a very unusual name."

For a moment I was convinced he meant something else entirely, then I remembered that, thanks to my recent experiences with Rose, I couldn't even trust my own thoughts any more let alone someone else's, so I changed the subject. For the rest of the meal we talked about the house next door to ours. Robbie told us how the nameless Americans were going to transform it into a house of such beauty that, just by living next door to them, our own cottage would double in price. Daniel laughed when he heard this.

"Except we don't want to sell it, do we, Rachel?'

I shook my head, mute as I thought what more money would mean to us. Despite me fighting it, I knew the rent from the rooms over the shop was going to make life a bit easier, and now it seemed as if our new neighbors were going to help us make our fortune. Well, maybe fortune was a bit optimistic, but according to Robbie it would make us enough money to spread our wings a bit if we ever decided to sell. At the very least we could holiday somewhere exotic and experience how Ella lived every day of her life. I wondered whether I would ever be able to persuade Daniel to consider the idea.

* * *

"So you already know Robbie Parker," Daniel said as he reversed the car out of the car park.

I shrugged. "Not really. He asked for a glass of water one day when he had been knocking things about a bit, and because he looked really hot I offered him a beer instead."

"It'll be interesting to see next door when it's finished although I'm afraid our cottage is going to look a bit pathetic beside it."

I didn't tell him I had already seen the plans and was green with envy. Instead I just shrugged again and turned to talk to Leah who was securely strapped into her baby seat behind us.

When I turned back to the front again the car was just beginning to climb Packhorse Hill. I frowned. "Where are we going?"

"I think it's time we shared some of our memories with Leah, don't you?"

I laughed, and Robbie, Millie, and the house next door were all forgotten as I tuned into Daniel's quirky take on fatherhood. "Personally I think she's a bit young although they do say children grow up faster these days."

He chuckled as our old car made that peculiar whining noise it always makes when it approaches the brow of a hill. "Not Leah. We're going to keep her locked up until she's at least twenty-five."

"A bit different from me then."

He glanced across at me and I could tell from the expression on his face that we were caught up in the middle of the same memories: me at sixteen, hanging around the shop waiting for Daniel to finish in the days when he was still an assistant, and then both of us lost for words as I pretended I was just passing; or me at seventeen refusing to consider any job unless it was close to Mapleby and Daniel. There were other memories too, more intimate ones. Daniel and me sharing our first kiss behind the barn when he walked me home from the cinema. The first time we made love, in a sunlit hollow at the top of Packhorse Hill, our suntanned legs sprawled across the blanket we had brought specially.

"Ah, but you matured exceptionally early," he teased as we trundled down a rough track towards our past. When he finally stopped the car we unclipped our seat belts and turned to look at one another.

"You've hardly changed at all, you know," Daniel reached out a hand and traced the curve of my lips before letting his fingers dip further, to the scooped neckline of my t-shirt. As they whispered across my skin I felt a tide of passion rising and suddenly I was eighteen again, and unable to think about anything except making love to Daniel. He saw it in my eyes as he leaned forward to kiss me.

"Bringing Leah was a mistake," he murmured. "We should have left her with your mother."

From behind us Leah gurgled her agreement and we drew apart laughing. Showing our baby daughter some of the places where we had made our memories was one thing, demonstrating them to her was quite another.

* * *

We passed the rest of the afternoon sitting and admiring the view while Leah lay on a blanket and watched the leaves flutter overhead before turning her attention to her favorite pastime of trying to wriggle forward.

"We'll need to pick up a playpen from the barn soon because it won't be long before she's crawling," I told Daniel.

He watched her for a minute or so, his arm around my shoulder, which is where it had been for most of the afternoon. Then he jumped up and held out his hand. "There's no time like the present."

I let him pull me to my feet. He was right. It would be better to get Leah used to the playpen before she could crawl because then she might be happy to stay inside it while I did my chores. The thought of her careering around the cottage with no possibility of restraint didn't bear thinking about.

Between us we collected all the paraphernalia that comes with a small baby and returned to the car. Then, with Leah firmly strapped into her seat, Daniel pinned me to the side of the car and proceeded to kiss me so thoroughly that I wasn't in any doubt about what was going to happen between us once Leah was in bed and asleep. Enjoying the titillation, I let my hands and tongue match his promise until our daughter's impatient wail from inside the car brought us back to the here and now. With a rueful grin, Daniel slid into the driver's seat. "Maybe we could get her to use the playpen when we get home," he said.

We didn't though because, as is often the way in the Pavalak family, there was a crisis. This time it was Grandma. Apparently she'd had some sort of funny turn in the middle of her lunch and become so agitated that the nurse had been forced to call out the duty doctor. She had called Ma at the same time and asked her to come over straight away. By the time we rocked up at the farm, full of sunshine, passion and fresh air, Ma was on the phone to Pa giving him an update. Several of my sisters were sitting at the kitchen table and a posse of very noisy children were running riot in the garden. When I walked in Pa waved me over to where he was standing beside the sink as he continued to talk to Ma.

"You don't need to do that because she and Daniel have just arrived. I'll pass you over so you can tell her yourself."

Mystified, I took the phone. Ma sounded relieved on the other end. "Thank goodness you've turned up, Rachel. We've been calling your cell phone for hours."

"Sorry Ma, but we were on Packhorse Hill and there's no signal up there."

She wasn't interested. All she wanted to know was how soon I could get to the nursing home.

"I can come now,' I said, bewildered by the sudden urgency and aware, too, that at least one of my sisters was feeling aggrieved that it was me and not her who Grandma wanted.

* * *

When I reached the nursing home Ma was pacing up and down outside, her cell phone clamped to her ear. She cut the call when she saw me and came hurrying over to where I'd parked the car.

"She's on about Rose again," she said, "and as you're the only one who seems to have a clue what she's talking about, maybe you can decipher what she's trying to say.

My heart sank. I had managed to forget about Rose for the whole afternoon while Daniel and I began to pick up where we'd left off when Leah was born, but now, when every nerve ending in my body was taut with anticipation, Rose had come calling. I sighed as I followed Ma into the building. So much for romance. So much for passion.

Grandma was sitting up in bed, her eyes tight shut and her cheeks a hectic red. Her thin, blue-veined hands were plucking at the bed covers as she repeated a short phrase over and over again. Ma gestured towards her in despair. "She's been doing that since two o'clock this afternoon and nobody knows what she's trying to say."

I walked across the room and perched on the edge of the bed. "Hello Grandma. Has Rose been talking to you again?"

She opened her eyes immediately and stared at me. "Rose?"

"No, Grandma, it's Rachel. I'm Rachel."

She stopped pulling at the bedcovers and seized both my hands with surprising strength. "Rose is in trouble and she wants you to know."

Now I was at a loss too. I might be able to get Grandma to talk to me about Rose but it didn't mean I could decipher her cryptic messages. My confusion must have shown in my face because, with that sudden lucidity that occasionally visited her poor confused brain, she shook my hands impatiently. "Read it," she said, her voice as clear as a bell.

"So that's what she's been trying to say all afternoon," Ma said, coming to stand at the foot of the bed. "It's those damned diaries, Rachel. Why did you ever tell her about them?"

I knew I hadn't but I wasn't about to tell Ma that, any more than I was going to tell her that a woman from another century was visiting Leah as well as having conversations with Grandma? If I didn't want everyone to start to look at me sideways again then it was better keep everything to myself.

I patted Grandma's gnarly old fingers. "I'll read it," I promised and then watched the rosy flush fade from her cheeks as she fell asleep.

* * *

By the time Ma and I got back to the farm, Pa and my sisters had pulled together a scratch meal that mainly consisted of bread and cheese. I tucked in while Ma brought them up-to-date. When she finished, everyone except Daniel rounded on me. With my mouth full they had to wait for an explanation. When I gave it, I made it sound as plausible as possible.

"All I've done is shown her some of those old photos like the nurse suggested. Unfortunately, they seem to have triggered a fixation on Granny Rose."

I didn't need to say another word because Ma took over, explaining how I had found the diaries too, and talked to Gran about those as well. "And now it's all she thinks about," she said.

I didn't waste my breath trying to correct her.

"It really is too bad that you've stirred her up like this, Rachel. Surely you should have handed those diaries over to a professional, to someone who knows what they're doing." Hester seemed to be speaking for almost everyone sitting around the table because they all glared at me with varying degrees of disapproval. Ma, however, stood up for me.

"It's not Rachel's fault. She's just been doing what we all agreed, and she's already got more out of Grandma than any of the rest of us have in a long while."

"So what's going to happen now the damage is done?" Hester asked sourly, clinging onto her belief that it was somehow my fault regardless.

"I guess I'm going to carry on reading the diaries," I said, and reached for another piece of bread.

Chapter Eleven

We were late home of course so Leah was fractious because she had fallen asleep while we were still at the farm and had been woken up twice, once when we strapped her into her car seat, and then again when we got home. By the time I finally settled her, Daniel was half asleep in front of the television and I had all but forgotten that rush of passion from earlier in the afternoon in my eagerness to discover what had upset Grandma. I changed into my very unsexy pajamas, ignored the milk stain on my dressing gown, and headed for the kitchen where I'd put Rose's diaries in a drawer.

Opening one at random I noted with interest that the handwriting had changed yet again. Written in black ink, it was bolder somehow, more mature. I turned to the first page where Rose appeared to be continuing a conversation she had obviously started in an earlier entry.

2nd September

Arthur and I picked blackberries on Packhorse Hill today. May says I shouldn't waste my time on him because he isn't ambitious. Honestly, ever since she started walking out with Archie Meads she has an opinion about everything, including how I should live my life.

Arthur! Hadn't Ma said Rose's husband, my great-great-grandfather, was called Arthur? I put it back on the pile while I made a mug of cocoa for Daniel and one for me. Then balancing the whole lot on a tray, I carried it through to our small sitting room. Daniel was too engrossed in his program to do more than mutter his thanks but for once I didn't care because I was on a mission. Making myself comfortable on the sofa, I reached for the first diary and flicked through to the last page I'd read, the one where Rose was hoping she would eventually get a bedroom of her own.

Reading on I found the entries where May was now training to be a milliner.

May says she is learning how to make bonnets and hats in the latest fashion. She says Miss Acton gets pictures from one of the fashion houses in Paris and that her millinery creations (that is what May calls them) are in such demand that she finds May's help indispensable.

May is heaps better at sewing than me and much more interested in fashion too, so she loves it. I wouldn't. I would hate to be stuck inside a shop all day being polite to everyone.

I finished that notebook and was halfway through the second one before anything else of real interest happened.

I walked into the village with Mama today so I could help her carry the shopping. We set off early because she wanted to visit Aunt Mabel. Aunt Mabel doesn't like little girls listening to grown up conversation so she gave me a slice of cake and a mug of milk and shooed me into the garden. She said it was so I could have some fresh air but really it was so I couldn't hear whatever it was she and Ma wanted to talk about. I didn't care though because watching people passing by is much more interesting than sitting on her overstuffed sofa.

I know leaving my plate and mug balanced on the wall while I made a fuss of her stupid cat wasn't a very sensible thing to do, but I didn't think about it until the miserable thing suddenly scratched the back of my hand. It made me jump and I knocked everything to the ground. Fortunately, I was only using Aunt Mabel's old tin mug and plate from the kitchen so nothing broke. When I saw the puddle of milk spreading across the road I almost burst into tears though.

A boy who was kicking a stone down the street picked the plate and mug up and put them back on the wall. He said the cake was too dusty for me to eat but that the birds would enjoy it. The horrible cat was already busy licking up the spilled milk. We watched him for a while, then the boy reached into his pocket and pulled out a wizened apple. He looked a bit embarrassed as he held it out. I started to say we had much better ones at home but then I stopped myself and just said thank you because I could see how much he wanted me to have it.

His told me his name is Arthur.

The next few pages were full of mundane everyday stuff but then Arthur appeared again and I learned that his uncle was the village cobbler and Arthur was his apprentice.

In the next dozen or so entries I learned a lot more, including the fact that Arthur had recently moved to Mapleby from a small town in Dorset, so to Rose, who had never ventured outside the village, he was an exotic foreigner with a strange accent. She was amused by some of the words he used and teased him about them. She learned a lot about his family as well and faithfully reported it in her diary. Apparently Arthur was the middle one of five brothers who were all learning to mend shoes. His father was a cobbler too.

Arthur's uncle only has one daughter – no sons, although his uncle says it's not for lack of trying, whatever that means - so he asked Arthur's father if Arthur could be his apprentice. His father was delighted because he hasn't enough work for Arthur and all of his brothers. Arthur is pleased too because now he has his own room and a secure future as well.

Arthur says his uncle wants him to marry his cousin Mathilda when he is eighteen but he is going to refuse because she is older than him and a lot taller. Arthur is quite short but he is taller than me. Papa says all the best things come in small packages. I think Arthur agrees with him.

I was so absorbed in the past that I didn't notice how late it was until the sound of Daniel's snoring brought me back to the here and now. With a start I saw it was after midnight. Leah hadn't woken for her night feed. Hurrying through to the nursery I saw that after weeks of trying she had finally managed to wriggle forward so her head was only a few inches from the edge of the crib. She was fast asleep though, her cheeks rosy with warmth. Remembering everything I had learned from the baby clinic, I pulled back her top blanket. Too hot was as bad as too cold. Then I returned to the sitting room to wake Daniel.

"Leah seems to have given up her late night feed," I told him.

He stretched and yawned as he glanced at the clock. When he saw how late it was he frowned. "Why didn't you wake me before?"

"Because I was too busy reading Rose's diaries to notice the time," I said.

He stood up and switched off the television. "You're really into her, aren't you?"

I nodded. "I didn't realize reading about other people's lives could be so interesting, and because Rose never expected anyone to ever read her diaries, she wrote down all her thoughts."

"Does that mean you are learning all the family secrets?"

I laughed. "Not yet but I'm hopeful."

He slipped his arm around my shoulders and kissed the top of my head. "So thanks to Rose I'm forgiven for falling asleep in front of the television, am I?"

I snuggled into him, relishing the width of his chest but too tired to want to explore any further. "Totally forgiven because she is much more interesting."

With a growl of mock disgust, he chased me through to the bedroom and we fell onto the bed laughing. "Tomorrow I'm going to prove just how much more interesting I am than a teenage girl from over a hundred years ago,"

"Is that a promise or a threat?" I asked, still laughing, because this was the Daniel I had fallen in love with.

"Whichever you want it to be," he answered with a mock leer and within less than five minutes we were asleep, tangled in one other's arms.

* * *

We woke late so Daniel rushed off without any breakfast or even a goodbye kiss, leaving Leah and me staring at one another over her bowl of porridge and wondering how to fill our day. Although I tried to hang onto Sunday's mood it faded when I saw the pile of washing we had generated over the weekend, so I was thoroughly fed up by the time I popped Leah back into her crib for her morning sleep. I only began to feel a bit more cheerful when I saw Robbie Parker backing his van into next door's driveway. Ignoring what Rose and my conscience said, I leaned out of the window.

"Coffee's brewing if you'd like some."

He waved his acceptance and arrived at the back door five minutes later carrying two jam doughnuts in a paper bag. I took them from him and tipped them onto a plate. He grinned at me.

"I always live in hope."

I knew I should ignore him. Instead I slanted him a shameless glance as I handed him a mug of coffee. "I hope you like it. It's a Columbian mix, hot and full bodied," I said.

He almost choked on his doughnut, and if Leah hadn't chosen that exact moment to cry out I'm not sure what would have happened next. Leaving him to lick the jam off his fingers I hurried through to the nursery. Rose was there and something in her eyes told me that Leah's tears hadn't been spontaneous. Without finding it odd that I was furious with a ghost, I turned on her.

"What did you do?" I hissed, picking up my daughter. Leah, her eyelashes still wet with tears, gave me her familiar goofy grin, while Rose did her usual disappearing trick.

I carried Leah through to the kitchen where Robbie was just finishing his coffee. He drained the mug and set it on the table. "Thanks Rachel. I'll bring iced buns tomorrow."

"So there's going to be a tomorrow, is there?" I asked him, my heart beating fast at my own boldness.

He grinned. "You know fine well there is. You still have to educate me about Mapleby and I have to persuade you to spread your wings a bit, and both of those things will take about the same amount of time it takes to renovate a house."

I watched him walk down the path, enjoying the slight swagger in his step and being far too interested in the width of his shoulders and the way his biceps flexed as he opened the gate. I doubted I had the courage to take up the promise in his eyes but it was going to be fun finding out.

* * *

"Cooee! Where are you Rachel?" It was Rebecca, the sister next in age to me. We argue the most but deep down she is the sister I love the best. Although she is six years older than me, at least we were born in the same decade, which meant we bonded over the music and fashion of our teenage years. It was Rebecca who bought me my first lip gloss and showed me how to use it. She bought me other things too when she started working. Nothing expensive, but still brilliant, like the glittery T-shirt that Ma said was trashy and too old for me, but which I wore non-stop until my rapidly developing breasts threatened to burst out of it.

Rebecca was the sister who had spent most time with me when I was depressed too, and she was the one who had told me not to be silly when I said I was a rubbish mother. Having babies hadn't affected her the same way; in fact, I'd go so far as to say she is a natural, but she had still been sympathetic, even when I resisted taking Leah for a walk.

101

"I'll come with you," she said. "Come on Rachel, just twenty minutes in the fresh air will do you good."

Of course she was right and I really believe that without her it would have taken me much longer to recover, so when I heard her calling I felt a warm rush of relief. Rebecca would take my mind off Robbie Parker and I could have a good bitch about Millie Carter, too. Maybe I could tell her about Rose as well.

"I'm in the kitchen," I called. "Have you come for lunch?"

"Not really, but you could persuade me," she rushed into the kitchen at her normal breathless pace, plucked Leah from my arms and smothered her with kisses. Then she grinned at me.

"Just getting my baby fix."

"John is still saying no to another one, then?"

She nodded. "He says three boys is two too many and that as it's impossible to guarantee a girl, we're done."

"And you...?"

She grinned again. "I'm working on it."

Still laughing at her, I opened a jar of sweet potato mush, popped it into the microwave and handed her one of Leah's special plastic spoons. "If you want another baby that much you can practice on your youngest niece while I make lunch. We'll eat outside under the cherry tree."

* * *

"So what's this I hear about you having stirred up Grandma?" Rebecca asked as we tucked into our ham salad, courtesy of the out-of-date food Daniel had brought home on Saturday.

I sighed. "You've been talking to Hester, haven't you? I've only been doing what the people at the nursing home suggested, and it's working. Grandma has remembered a lot of things and some of them are really interesting."

"Such as?"

And before I knew it I was telling her all about Rose. Not that I had seen her ghost or anything, I knew better than that, but I told her everything I knew about the cottage and Rose's life up until she met Arthur.

Her eyes lit up with enthusiasm. "Have you still got the diaries or are they at the nursing home?"

"They're right here," I slid open the kitchen drawer to show her. She seized one and flicked through the pages.

"God Rachel, her writing is miniscule. Are you really going to read the whole lot?"

I nodded. "I can't stop now I know that our great-great-grandmother lived here when she was a girl, and that next door is built on what was once part of our garden. And the old horse that died that I told you about, well I've even found his horseshoe. It's nailed to the fence as a sort of memorial. Come on I'll show you."

I unstrapped Leah from her highchair and hoisted her onto my hip. Then, with Rebecca following, I hurried down the path towards next door's gate.

Robbie must have seen us coming because by the time we got there he was leaning against the open kitchen door, grinning. "So it's conducted tours now, is it?"

I introduced him to Rebecca, wishing with all my heart that he hadn't stripped to the waist since I last saw him. My sister didn't have any such qualms. She openly ogled him while I explained what I wanted to show her. Although he didn't seem to notice, he did grab his T-shirt and pull it over his head before he led us around the side of the house to look at the fence. The damage was done though. I had already seen the long curve of his back and the taut muscles across his stomach. I had seen the tan too. It wasn't just his face and arms that were brown. It was all of him. My stomach flipped at what that might mean. With an effort I concentrated on what he was saying.

"Looking is not a problem Rachel, but be careful because a building site is dangerous."

It took me a moment to realize he was referring to the pile of rubble that had accumulated at the back of the house since my last visit and not to the unexpected thrill of his naked chest. I nodded, knowing from the glint in Rebecca's eye that she was enjoying my embarrassment.

"Looking can be dangerous too," she murmured as we skirted a newly delivered pile of breeze blocks and then let Robbie help us across the old rotting planks beside the fence.

I ignored her.

"If this is what you're looking for then it's just as well you've come today because I'm pulling the fence down tomorrow so the contractors can get their machinery in," Robbie stopped beside the horseshoe.

"Rose isn't going to like that," I said before I could stop myself.

Robbie and Rebecca both stared at me as I stuttered my way into a better explanation. "What I mean is that I don't want you to take it down because it's history. That horse-shoe was put up there by my great-great-grandmother when she was about twelve years old."

Rebecca laughed as she leaned closer so she could read the words burned into the wood. "Those diaries seem to be getting to you, Rachel."

Seeing Robbie's confusion, I told him about the diaries and how I had discovered the story of the horse-shoe. Although he was interested he still shook his head. "Sorry Rachel, but it has to come down. I'll save the horse-shoe for you if you want though."

I shrugged as if it was of no account and then the three of us turned and clambered back the way we had come. When we reached the path I apologized for interrupting his work.

"It's not a problem," he said, and then he told us that his mother had been researching her own family tree for ages. "Although I think she's stuck on her great-grandfather, or maybe it's her great-great-grandfather, I don't exactly remember."

"You mean you weren't really listening when she told you," Rebecca teased him.

He grinned at her. "Something like that, although now I've seen how excited you both are about that horse-shoe, perhaps I'll take a bit more interest."

"From now on I might be calling in on a regular basis," Rebecca whispered, slanting a wicked look in Robbie's direction as she kissed me goodbye.

I pinched her. "If you do, I'll tell that long suffering husband of yours."

"As if." She climbed into her car laughing. "We Pavalak girls have to stick together when it comes to eye candy. Keep at those diaries Rachel, and let me know what else you find out."

Leah and I waved her away and then ignoring the fact that Robbie was leaning against the fence, shirtless again and with his his cell phone clamped to his ear, I walked back into the cottage.

Rose was waiting for me, only this time it was another Rose altogether. She was dressed in a nut brown dress and her dark curls were piled onto the top of her head. Gone was the little girl with the blue ribbon in her hair. She was still young though. About seventeen I would think. She was sitting at the kitchen table swinging her feet, and her tongue was pressed between pearly teeth as she concentrated on what she was writing. I peered over her shoulder.

May is getting married and I am to be bridesmaid. I will wear my best dress and Mama is to sew me a new sash. May is having a brand new dress, and she is going to wear a new hat as well. She says it is Miss Acton's wedding present to her and is in the very latest fashion. I haven't seen it yet but it's bound to be elegant because May wouldn't wear anything else. I think it's stupid that she has to stop working as soon as she is a married woman, but she doesn't seem to mind. She says learning to be a milliner was a means to an end, which is her way of saying she would never have met someone as rich as Archie if she had just worked as a maid like most of the other girls around here.

I am never going to work as a maid, or in a shop. I'm going to stay home and help Mama until Arthur has saved up enough money to marry me. By then I will have learned everything I need to know about keeping house. May will have servants to help her up at the big house, but I want to do it all by myself, the same as Mama.

At the sound of footsteps on the garden path, Rose slammed the notebook shut and hid it in the apron she was wearing over her dress, and by the time her mother and May entered the kitchen she was busy scraping carrots at the sink in the scullery. When they called her she hurried through, acting all surprised as if she hadn't heard a thing.

"There you are, Rose," her mother plumped herself onto a kitchen chair with a sigh of relief. She was flushed and a bit out of breath but she was smiling. "Come and see May's hat. It's a marvel of flowers and feathers and far too good for the likes of us."

"Not for Archie's family though, Mama," May scolded, her lips drawn tight as purse strings.

Her mother laughed as she patted her arm. "I'm only teasing, lovey. You must learn not to take everything so seriously." Then she turned back to Rose. "Boil the water for some tea, and while we're waiting May can parade her finery."

For a moment May looked about to refuse but then she relaxed and soon she was as excited as any modern day bride-to-be as she carefully opened the lid of the hat box she had placed on the kitchen table. The veiled confection she lifted out was indeed a marvel. The froth of tiny white flowers clambering around the pale straw crown looked real and so did the hint of green leaves peeping from beneath them.

"Miss Acton copied it from a picture she saw in a fashion magazine," she told Rose as she adjusted the hat to a becoming angle and then peered at her distorted reflection in the shiny surface of the copper pan hanging over the

106

range. "She says white flowers are the latest thing for brides."

It was clear that Rose was impressed even though she tried hard not to show it. She screwed up her face into a frown as May twisted and twirled in front of her. "You'll never be able to wear it again though will you, not once you're a married woman, not if white is just for brides."

May gave her a withering glance. "Honestly Rose, you really are stupid at times. Of course I'll be able to wear it again, I'll just add some colored flowers and match them to whatever outfit I'm wearing."

Their mother, no doubt as used to deflecting an argument as Ma was, picked up a brown paper parcel from beside her chair, untied the string that secured it, and shook out a length of pale blue organza. "Look what we bought for your sash, Rose."

"And I'm going to sew tiny blue flowers onto a ribbon for your hair," May added. Her cheeks were pink with excitement and so, too, were Rose's. She reached out and smoothed her fingers across the organza.

I knew she was imagining how pretty she would look in her best dress on May's wedding day. I wondered if Arthur was going to be invited and, while I was wondering, the kitchen flipped back to normal and I found myself sitting at my own table with Leah gurgling away happily on my lap.

Chapter Twelve

I thought about May's wedding while I changed Leah's nappy and by the time she was clean and dry I had decided to take her for an afternoon walk via the church. Although I rarely visited it nowadays, I had spent a lot of my childhood sitting on its dark wooden pews daydreaming instead of listening to the vicar's endless sermons.

Robbie shouted a greeting as I pushed Leah's pram down the path and through the gate. I gave a half-hearted wave in return, my mind too full of May's wedding day and Rose's blue sash to be distracted by his lean torso for more than half a minute. Besides, Rebecca's reaction to his very obvious masculine charms had convinced me I was just the latest in a long line of slightly bored housewives to fall for him, and that I needed to pull myself together before things went too far.

I was still telling myself this when I reached the church. As was usual for mid afternoon on a Monday, it was empty. I hesitated in the porch, not sure whether I should unstrap Leah or just push the pram inside. While I was dithering, the heavy wooden door opened and I found myself face to face with the vicar. He solved my dilemma by holding it wide and then following me back inside. He had only been in the parish for a few months so I didn't really know him.

"It's Rachel, isn't it? You're married to Daniel who runs the village shop."

I nodded, embarrassed, as I muttered that I still had to organize a date for Leah's baptism.

He smiled. "I'm sure you'll get around to it soon. You can get me at the vicarage any day between four and six."

I gave him a startled look. "Any day?"

He chuckled. "It's sort of goes with the job, although my wife fights it from time to time.

"Well, I'm with your wife," I told him. "At least Daniel has Sunday free."

His eyes twinkled. "My busiest day, I'm afraid."

I laughed. "I suppose it is."

We looked at one another appraisingly, the vicar waiting to see if I needed his advice, and me hesitating to tell him why I was there. Eventually I took a deep breath and explained about Rose and May, and all the information I had found in the diaries.

Long before I finished he began to usher me down the aisle. I dropped my voice to a whisper as my words began to echo around the empty church. Leah, her eyes wide as she stared up at the bright colors in the stained glass windows, remained uncharacteristically silent.

He smiled at me. "You don't have to worry about making a noise when there's nobody else here, you know. The church is a joyous place. Look at how the sun is lighting up the altar, and how the air is heady with the scent of flowers overlaid with centuries of furniture polish, and tell me we have to be serious. You can't, can you?"

I shook my head. He was right although I'd never seen it before. This small church was the centerpiece of the village, a place where nearly everyone who lived in Mapleby was baptized, married and buried. It was where generations of children had learned their first lisping prayers and sung songs that involved a lot of clapping and hand gestures. It was where Rose had gone every Sunday wearing her best dress, and where she had probably got married too, just like Daniel and me. I wondered why I hadn't thought about it before, why I hadn't searched for her grave in the churchyard, or done what I was about to do now, and search through the parish records.

The vicar's smile grew wider as he led me through to the vestry. "My name is James by the way, James Carroll, and I'm delighted you agree with me. Now remind me again of your Great Aunt's name."

"Great-great Aunt," I corrected him. "And her name was May...um...er," I ground to a halt as I searched back in my memory. Did I even know her surname? Then I remembered Rose's first entry in her diary. "It was Petty," I told him. "May Petty."

He nodded as he unearthed a heavy book from the depths of a dusty wooden chest and lifted it onto the vestry table. Within minutes he had found the right entry. We bent over it together, peering at the faded copperplate writing.

May Agnes Petty, spinster and milliner, aged 23, and Archibald Edward Meads, bachelor and jeweler, aged 30, both resident in the parish of Mapleby, were married on this 20th day of April, 1887.

The entry noted that Archie's father was also a jeweler and that May's father was an ostler. Seeing the puzzlement on my face, James Carroll explained that an ostler was someone who cared for horses.

"That's right, her father looked after the horses at the big house," I agreed excitedly as I recalled exactly how Rose and May's father had looked, right down to the cap he wore tilted rakishly on his head, and the red kerchief knotted at his throat.

"Originally ostlers were the men who cared for the horses at coaching inns but the term changed through common usage until it came to mean anyone who looked after horses," the vicar looked as thrilled as I felt.

I hesitated. "Do you have time…that is, could we look for another entry, only this time I don't know the year?"

"Hmm, not so easy, but the parish was a lot smaller then so it probably won't take very long. Can you whittle it down to say a five-year period?"

I thought for a moment. Although Rose seemed to be at least five years younger than May she already had a beau who, by the time of May's wedding must have almost finished his apprenticeship. Did this mean that Rose got married while she was still in her teens? I doubted it, given how protective her parents were, but she might have married Arthur as soon as she was twenty-one. I counted up the years in my head and gave him a range to work through. Then I unstrapped Leah from her pram and carried her slowly around the church, showing her all the pictures and letting her rub her plump little fingers on the carved figures while he searched through the register. I hurried back to the vestry when a shout of delight told me he had struck gold.

He pointed to the first entry at the top of a page.

Rose Eliza Petty, spinster, aged 21, and Arthur Randolph Davis, bachelor and cobbler, aged 24, both of the parish of Mapleby, were married this 18th day of August in the year 1891.

No occupation was noted for Rose so she really had stayed at home and helped her mother until she married. I hoped it had turned her into better housewife than she had ever shown signs of being when she was younger. Arthur's father was also listed as a cobbler and Rose's father was an ostler, as before.

I thanked James Carroll, even as I wondered what Rose had worn on her wedding day. Maybe May had loaned her a hat, or maybe she had been able to afford a new dress of her own by then. Somehow I doubted it though. Still, at least I knew when she and Arthur had married, so now I could flick through the diaries until I found the correct date.

Locking away the huge book in the parish chest, the vicar led me through the vestry and out of the church into the sunshine. We smiled at one another and I promised to call at the vicarage to fix a date for Leah's baptism. Then, just as I was turning away, he spoilt it all.

"Please thank Daniel for his donation to the church fete. I was going call into the shop and thank him myself, but if you would pass the message on I'd be very grateful."

"I will." Donating stuff for the raffle that took place every year at the church fete was part and parcel of owning the village shop. It was expected of us, and in return we were allowed to run a stall where we sold the sweets and drinks that Daniel got discounted from the wholesaler. It was the next bit that took my breath away.

"And what he's doing...what you are both doing for Millie Carter is even more generous. Most people would have called the police when they caught her shoplifting, so to offer her a job instead was a truly Christian act. And when she told me she's going to move into the rooms over the shop as soon as they have been decorated I felt as if I was witnessing a modern day miracle."

He obviously thought I knew everything there was to know about Millie Carter and that I was part of all those so-called Christian acts that were saving her from ruin. That would be because he had the sort of marriage where he and his wife told one another everything, of course. It obviously hadn't occurred to him that someone as generous as Daniel would fail to mention the small matter of shoplifting to his wife, so he had no idea that he had just betrayed Millie, and Daniel too. I watched him walk away with my farewell smile still pasted on my face but it didn't last. As soon as I turned for home I started scowling and I was still scowling when my generous husband arrived home for his evening meal.

* * *

"When were you going to tell me?" I raged as I slammed a plate of pasta down in front of him. Leah was already in bed and asleep. I'd made sure of that because I wanted to be able to shout and stamp without upsetting her.

Picking up his fork, Daniel shook his head wearily. "When I thought you were ready to have a civilized conversation about it."

"Oh, so it's my fault is it? I'm the uncivilized one, not Millie Carter the thief."

He put his fork down again and looked at me. "Come on Rachel, you're better than that. You've known Millie forever so you know what sort of a life she's had. Taking a couple of cans of meat and a pack of tomatoes was an act of desperation, not the beginning of a slide into crime."

"How do you know that? Our shop might be one of many. Her house might be stacked out with canned meat and tomatoes." I knew how ridiculous I sounded but I couldn't stop myself.

"So if Leah was hungry and your larder was empty, you would just let her cry herself to sleep, would you?" Daniel's tone should have stopped me in my tracks but I'm nothing if not consistent.

"So that was her story, was it? She certainly knows how to play you, doesn't she? Two hungry children, no job, nowhere to live…you always were a sucker Daniel, I just didn't realize how big a sucker until now."

"Will you listen to yourself Rachel, and then tell me you like what you hear," his voice was tight with anger as he slammed his hands on the table and stood up, knocking his chair over in his hurry to put as much distance as possible between us. When he reached the door he turned and looked at me, and I suddenly saw myself through his eyes. It was too late to do a thing about it though so I let him go without another word.

* * *

I pretended to be asleep when Daniel eventually returned home around midnight. I doubt if my heavy breathing convinced him because ever since Leah was born I've woken up at the slightest sound. At least he didn't speak though.

He didn't speak the following morning either, except to grunt a goodbye as he slammed the door behind him. It bothered me more than I was prepared to admit because Daniel never holds a grudge. I wondered if I ought to call at the shop and be nice to Millie, talk to her about her children or something. I was still mulling it over when a thought struck me. What if all this 'let's rescue poor Millie stuff' was just a ruse, something she and Daniel had cooked up so they could spend time together without it looking suspicious? What if he was in love with her and preparing to move into the rooms over the shop himself when it was finished?

I knew I was being irrational but the thought sent an icy shiver down my back. Millie Carter is what is commonly known as a stunner. Even after two children her curves are all in the right places and her thick auburn hair hangs to her waist when she shakes out her trademark ponytail. She's pretty too, much prettier than me, with long hazel eyes under perfectly arched brows, a straight nose, and lips that always look as if they are waiting to be kissed. In all conscience I couldn't really blame Daniel if he fancied her, not after all I'd put him through in the past six months.

I was still mulling this over when Robbie tapped on the kitchen door. Without thinking I pulled it open, forgetting I was still wearing pajamas. He backed away when he saw me.

"Sorry, I didn't realize it was so early. I'll come back later."

My eyes followed his gaze and I saw I had forgotten to refasten the top buttons of my pajama jacket when I finished giving Leah her morning feed. Flushing, I pulled it close. "No, it's me. I've been up for hours; I just haven't gotten around to getting dressed yet."

He held out a paper bag. "Iced buns as promised."

I took them. "Thank you. Give me five minutes to throw on some clothes and I'll make coffee."

"Are you sure? You look harassed."

I gave a bitter laugh. "Harassed is only the half of it. Come on in and sit down because I'm fed up with my own company."

* * *

By the time I had dressed, splashed cold water on my face, and finger combed my hair into some semblance of a style, Robbie had made two mugs of coffee and found a plate for the buns. I picked one up and started to lick the icing off with the tip of my tongue. When I saw Robbie watching me I decided to bite it instead.

"A trouble shared is a trouble halved," he said, his eyes serious as he regarded me across the rim of his coffee mug.

I shook my head. I might be furious with Daniel but I wasn't about to be disloyal to him. I could, however, ask Robbie about the shop. Maybe that way I'd get an insight into what was actually going on.

"How is the decorating?"

He squinted at me and decided I wasn't going to talk about anything else. "Fine. It's mostly just white on white, so really easy to do. Apart from the bathroom it should be finished by the end of the week."

"So soon?" My satisfying if unrealistic vision of Millie Carter being homeless for months faded.

He nodded and then started to talk about next door and how he had already taken the fence down. "I was careful with the horse-shoe though. If you like I'll bring it round. I could even fix it to your fence as a feature if that's what you want."

"Thank you, I'd love that.' He had said exactly the right thing to make me forget about Daniel and Millie. When he saw how much it had cheered me up he offered to fetch it there and then.

I was pouring a second cup of coffee for each of us when he returned and he smiled his thanks as he put the horse-shoe on the kitchen table. I ran my finger over its knobbly surface which was pitted in places with rust. It was never going to be a thing of beauty but the history it invoked was priceless.

"I'd love for you to fix it onto my fence." I told him.

"I can do better than that. If you'll give me a day or two I can use the old fencing panel to fashion some sort of memorial plaque so you don't lose the words and the little heart that was burnt into the wood."

For a moment I was speechless with gratitude, then I opened the drawer where I kept Rose's diaries and scrabbled beneath them for the envelope full of photos.

Tipping them onto the table I sorted through until I found one of Rose. "That's her," I said. "She's the girl who put up the horse-shoe, only she was much younger then. This photo was taken years later when she was a young woman."

He picked it up and studied it. "She looks like you."

"That's what my Grandma says."

"You mean there's still someone alive who knew her?"

I nodded as I began to tidy the photos away. "Yes. The woman in this photo is my grandmother's grandmother, which makes her my great-great-grandmother. She was still alive when my Grandma was born although by then she was a very old woman."

"And here she is again," he picked up another photo of Rose, the one where she was making everyone laugh at some sort of party. "Who are these people?"

I shrugged as I pointed at the man I now knew to be Arthur. "He's her husband and I think little girl belongs to her. The rest must be friends."

"So are they at a wedding or is it a party, or a picnic?"

I shook my head, surprised by his interest. "I've absolutely no idea. It's fascinating though isn't it? All those people laughing and enjoying themselves and we'll never know what they said or why they were together."

He was still staring intently at the photo when I became aware that we were standing closer together than was strictly necessary and moved away. It broke the spell and moments later he left, promising to return with the horse-shoe mounted on a plaque as soon as he had time to make it.

Pushing the photos back into to their envelope I lingered over the one that had so transfixed Robbie, and studied the people directly behind Rose. There were three men and two women sitting close together and all laughing. Standing to one side, behind Arthur so out of his line of vision, was another man. He was tall and dark and vaguely familiar. He was the only one not laughing. Instead he was looking directly at Rose with what I can only describe as an expression of longing. I stared at him for ages wishing that the photo was just a little less faded because then I would be able to tell if she was returning his gaze.

Feeling more troubled than I had any right to be, I decided it would be a good day to visit Grandma again. Small babies need a daily dose of fresh air, and with so few distractions in Mapleby, taking Leah to the nursing home almost every day wasn't anything to be remarked upon.

* * *

If anything, the weather was hotter than ever, which meant Robbie was stripped to the waist again when I walked past next door pushing Leah in her pram. Fortunately for my peace of mind, he was too busy directing the contractors to see me, although the lorry driver looked me up and down and whistled long and low under his breath.

Secretly I was flattered. Now I spent most of every day in the cottage on my own, I was prepared to take any compliments I could get. I pretended I hadn't heard him though, the same as I pretended I hadn't noticed that Robbie was bare to the waist again. I couldn't ignore how I felt about Daniel's behavior however, or mine either, even though I tried my hardest, and my walk to the nursing home was miserable.

When I got there and peeped in on Grandma, she was asleep. "I'm not in a hurry so I'll take Leah to sit the garden for half-an-hour," I told the nurse on duty.

Nodding her approval, she said Grandma would probably be awake by then and left me to it. I opened the glass doors that led out to the small formal garden, and unstrapping Leah, I picked her up and walked towards the small bronze sundial in the centre. Just before I reached it I heard laughter from beyond the retaining wall, and the shrieking of excited children. Changing direction, I peered over the top.

Below the wall, grass sloped away in a rolling lawn until, in the far distance, it was stopped abruptly by a river bank thick with reeds. I blinked. Where was the car park and the narrow approach road with its exit and entry signs?

Then I saw the children. There were at least five of them of varying ages and they were playing tag. Two women sat on a seat nearby. Closer to my vantage point a man dressed in what appeared to be evening dress was supervising two young girls as they set dishes on a long table in the shade of a towering horse chestnut tree. It wasn't until he approached the women and spoke to one of them in a deferential tone that I realized he was a butler and that the girls dressed in black were maids.

Although I strained my ears I couldn't hear their conversation but I understood the body language, so I wasn't really surprised when, moments later, a woman dressed somberly in brown appeared from somewhere behind me, and called to the children. She was obviously the nanny, and although they protested and carried on pushing one another, they obeyed her summons. Within minutes they were sitting around the table, quieter now except for an occasional outbreak of giggles.

The two other women joined them. I could see them more clearly now they were closer to the wall, and with a shock I recognized a very different Rose. She was pale and the expression on her face could only be described as haunted. She was also plumper than I remembered, and when she reached across the table to wipe a smudge from a child's nose I realized she was pregnant. I stared at her, taking in the dark circles under her eyes and the new lines at the corner of her mouth. Was she ill? Was her pregnancy too much for her?

"May I have more lemonade?" One of the children, a girl of about eight years old, spoke to her.

Half rising to reach for the jug, Rose was interrupted by the nanny beckoning to one of the maids. With remarkable promptness she filled the little girl's glass and then walked around the table checking on the needs of the rest of the children. When she had finished Rose gave a weak smile and thanked her. The other woman, who hadn't spoken until then, frowned at her.

"You're here for a rest, Rose, not to pander to the children."

Looking a picture of embarrassed misery, Rose shook her head. "You know it takes me a day or two to get used to it, May."

May's expression softened. "I know, but you must. And you must have a nap after lunch as well, and enjoy breakfast in bed. The doctor says you need complete rest so that's what you're going to have."

I thought for a moment that Rose was going to cry but she didn't. Instead she gave her sister a look that was a mixture of gratitude and resignation, and returned to her lunch. She only picked at her food though and soon May was scolding her again.

"Eat up, do. You're setting the children a bad example by pushing food around your plate like that."

Her comment made Rose laugh and the laughter brought a tinge of pink to her cheeks as she gestured towards the children. "Nothing is going to stop mine from eating. Look how they are tucking in. You would think they hadn't been fed for a week."

"That's because Auntie May has better cakes than us, and softer bread," the girl who had asked for more lemonade told her.

"And she always has peaches and cream," a younger girl added, spooning up a last mouthful from the bowl in front of her. "Why don't we have peaches, Mama? Is it because they are too expensive?"

"It's because Uncle Archie has a hot house," Rose told her. "And a gardener who knows how to grow peaches as well."

"And I'm lucky enough to have a cook who knows how to preserve them too so we can eat them all year," May added. "Now if you've all finished you can go indoors with Nanny to wash your hands and faces and then you may play with the dressing up clothes in the attic until bedtime."

"The attic, the attic, we love the attic," the children chanted as they tumbled off their chairs and raced towards the house with the long suffering nanny following behind.

"I should have made them say thank you but I don't seem to have the energy for anything these days," Rose sighed as she watched them disappear into the house.

May waited until the maid had refilled their teacups and then waved her away, saying she could come back later to clear the table. She didn't speak again until the girl was out of earshot, then she turned to her sister with a frown. "This has to stop Rose. You need to pull yourself together before questions are asked."

This time the tears that had been brimming in Rose's eyes spilled over. "I wish I could but I don't know how."

"You just need to set your mind to it," May said, her sympathetic expression at odds with the harshness of her voice. "At the very least there are the children to think of, but there's Arthur too. When I asked you what he's done to deserve this, your answer made no sense. How can somebody be too kind?"

"I...I can't explain," Rose was really sobbing now. "Besides, even if I could you would just tell me to stop being so silly."

"Not necessarily, not if it's to do with him giving away money again. Is it to do with money?"

"Yes. He still gives away every spare penny we have. I try not to begrudge helping his sisters because they are both spinsters and they find life hard, but I get angry when he mends people's shoes for free or tells them to pay when they can. He even patched up a pair of boots in exchange for a dozen eggs last week, all the time knowing full well that we have plenty of laying hens of our own. If you didn't give me the clothes your children have grown out of I don't know how we would manage."

"Well, they are no good to me as I certainly don't intend to have another baby. I've told Archie very firmly that that bit of our life is over."

Rose stared at her, her own woes forgotten for a moment. "You never have. Whatever did he say?"

Her sister shrugged. "Nothing. He was too busy checking his accounts. I knew what he was like when I married him though, so I can hardly complain when he mostly ignores me. Besides he is very generous and he fully expects to keep me in the manner to which I have become very accustomed."

"I do admire your pragmatism May. I wish I could be the same. Instead I was so determined to marry for love that I never gave money a thought, and look where it's got me," Rose's sigh came from somewhere deep inside her. "And now this. If we could even afford just a little bit of luxury, I might not have had my head turned. And now I'm going to break Arthur's heart, which he doesn't deserve even if he gives all our money away."

With a sharp intake of breath May leaned across the table and took her sister's hands. "Now listen to me Rose, and listen carefully. You are not going to break Arthur's heart because he is never going to know the truth. This baby you are expecting is a blessing, not a punishment, because it's brought you to your senses. Arthur will love it just the same as he loves Joyce and Molly, so why upset him? You know you and the children are his whole world, so to destroy it would be the worst cruelty."

Rose started to cry again. "But what if he finds out?"

"He's not going to, is he, not unless you tell him, because I'm certainly not going to, and the only other person who might suspect the truth is long gone, back to his tea plantation in India."

"But it means living a lie for the rest of my life."

"I know but surely that's better than…

* * *

"She's awake now." Behind me I could hear the nurse calling. I half turned to let her know I'd heard her, and when I next looked over the wall all I could see was a row of neatly parked cars, a couple of wheelie bins and a large exit sign.

* * *

Grandma was sitting in a chair by the window when Leah and I joined her. She patted Leah's chubby hand and then spoke to me as if we were already in the middle of a conversation.

"It was a boy and she called him Robert. May told her not to. She said it would be better if she severed all ties, but Rose insisted. She said his father's name was the only bit of truth she could give him."

"And what about Arthur? Was he happy with the name?"

"Anything Rose wanted was fine with Arthur. She was the sun, the moon and the stars to him. Besides, he was glad to have a son after two girls."

"And Rose never told him?"

Gran shook her head. "Never. The deceit destroyed her, though. She was never the same after Robert was born and Arthur knew it, he just didn't know why."

I spread Leah's blanket on the floor and plonked her down, scattering some of her toys around her so she had something to aim for when she started squirming forward. Gran watched, smiling, and didn't speak again until I asked her a question that was puzzling me.

"When did it stop being a secret?"

She shook her head so hard that the wispy curls on her forehead quivered. "Rose never told anyone."

"May then?"

"No. The secret died with them."

"So how come you know?"

But Gran's lucid moment had gone and in another minute she had nodded off to sleep again. I sat there, playing with Leah, until the care assistant arrived with two cups of tea, closely followed by the nurse. She raised her eyebrows in surprise.

"I was sure she was awake when I called you. I hope she hasn't been asleep all this time?"

I shook my head. "No, only for the last ten minutes or so. She was quite good before that."

Satisfied, she busied herself sorting through the various bottles of pills until she found the ones Grandma needed to take with her tea. I waited until she had counted them out before asking her a question

"Who owned this building before it became a nursing home?"

Even as I said it, I knew I was being stupid. A quick glance around was all that was needed for anyone to see it was purpose built, with long straight corridors for wheelchairs, big, airy modern windows for light and sunshine, and extra wide doorways with automatic doors to make things easier for everyone.

"What I mean is, who did the land belong to before it was built?" I bent down and tickled Leah to hide my embarrassment.

"The local council as far as I know."

"Before that it belonged to the Trayner family," an older care assistant said as she gently coaxed Gran awake. "They lived in a big house here for years and years until old Mr Trayner sold the whole estate to the council and the house was turned into offices."

The nurse joined in. "Of course, I remember now. It was ever so grand with columns and high windows and all sorts of carving."

The care assistant nodded. "The councilors liked it because sitting in an office overlooking the gardens made them feel important, but in the end it cost too much to run so they sold it to the highest bidder."

"And I suppose the gardens were where the car park is now?" I picked up Leah and carried her to the window.

"Yes, they were beautiful, and when Mr Trayner lived here they were ever so well cared for. He even grew peaches and pineapples in his greenhouse until he fell and broke his hip. After that it was all downhill, and it wasn't long before his son came down from London and took him away. Then the next thing we knew he had sold the whole lot to the council."

I stored the name Trayner for future reference and turned to where Grandma was just waking up. She peered at me and then at Leah. "Is that you Rose, and little Robert?"

"No Gran, it's Rachel and Leah, and we're going to leave you to drink your tea in peace. We'll be back though."

Chapter Thirteen

I was very thoughtful on my journey home. I had no idea why I was able to see through the mesh of time to where Rose still seemed to live but it didn't frighten me. Far more worrying was the thought that I would inadvertently blurt out what was happening to Daniel or Ma, or to one of my sisters, and they would drag me kicking and screaming back to Doctor Gove. I was so busy with my thoughts that I didn't notice the white van until it pulled up just ahead of me.

"Penny for them?" Robbie was sitting in the driving seat with the window wound down when I caught up with it.

"Not worth it," I said.

"What about a lift then? I'm going past your place and Leah's stroller will fit inside the van."

I shook my head. "No thanks, the walking is good for me. Besides you don't have a baby seat."

"Well spotted." The grin he gave me turned me gooey inside despite having promised myself that it wasn't going to happen again. He knew it and his eyes twinkled.

In an effort to distract myself I said the first thing that came into my head. "You're interested in Mapleby's local history aren't you? Well here's something for you. I learned today that there used to be a grand house where the nursing home is now."

He looked interested enough for me to continue, so I told him about the council offices and the lawns and the river. "They're not there now, not even the river. It's just a car park. I think the council must have built over it or something."

"Probably. I always think it's a shame when something like that happens. Did you learn anything about the family who lived there?"

"Only that they were called Trayner," I was going to keep everything I had learned about Rose and her sister very firmly to myself.

"Are you sure it was Trayner?" His sudden enthusiasm surprised me.

"Yes, I am, but as I've never heard of anyone called Trayner living in Mapleby I guess the whole family moved away years ago."

"Well guess what, they're coming back. The Americans are called Trayner…Marnie and Bob Trayner."

"You mean the people who own the house next to ours?" My voice rose a couple of octaves I was so excited.

He nodded. "And something even more weird has happened. My mother called me last night but she was so excited I could barely understand a word she said. Apparently she's found a family link with Mapleby. You remember I told you she was keen on genealogy, well now she wants me to do some digging for her. It seems she's discovered a letter to my great-great-grandfather from someone living here."

I stared at him. "You're kidding. What did it say?"

"I don't know because my cell battery ran out before she finished talking. I'll call her tonight to find out though, and I'll tell you tomorrow."

I watched him drive away, my mind in a turmoil. Rose, May, the Trayners, and now Robbie's great-great-grandfather. The past was beginning to take over the present. I wondered what Daniel would make of it and the thought made me quicken my step, eager to get home so I could tell him. Then I remembered that we still weren't speaking and decided I wouldn't tell him anything at all.

* * *

As it happened, talking to him wasn't a problem because when I reached home the note he had left on the table made it clear he had already been and gone. I screwed it up and

126

threw it in the trash. If he wanted to spend the evening helping Robbie to paint the flat so Millie Carter could move in even sooner than planned, then that was up to him. For my part I was going to search through Rose's diaries once Leah was in bed, to find out what had happened to her.

I started reading hunched over my solitary ready-meal, another one of Daniel's past the sell-by-date gifts that I had stuffed into the freezer in a fit of pique. Now though, it was useful, and if I'm honest, it was quite nice too. The mashed potato was topped with cheese, and the creamy sauce was full of tasty chunks of fish. I boiled a few peas and tipped them onto the plate beside it and then ate one-handed, turning the pages of Rose's diaries with my free hand.

I was still reading when I heard Daniel slam the car door and crunch his way across the gravel path. Despite behaving as if I was cramming for an exam I still hadn't discovered a single thing that my unplanned journeys into the past hadn't already shown me when, bingo, I saw something so unexpected it took my breath away. A reference to a Robert Parker.

Robert Parker! I was beyond speech when Daniel came into the room so I didn't answer when he spoke to me. I didn't even listen if the truth be told and that was what made him angry.

"For goodness sake Rachel, how long is this going to go on? You agreed we should decorate the flat so Millie can use it, you even chose the new bathroom fitments, so why must you make it into such a big thing?"

I shook my head. "It's not that…it's not about Millie…" but he had gone to have a shower, slamming the bathroom door behind him.

I knew I should pack away the books, put my congealed plate in the sink to soak, and then go and explain that I was so far from worrying about Millie at this moment that she could serve in the shop stark naked and I wouldn't care. I didn't, though, because Rose won out and I was feverishly hunting for more references to Robert Parker when Daniel came back into the room and turned on the TV without so much as a glance in my direction.

May and Archie are having a garden party and almost everyone in the village is going, even the children. Joyce is so excited and even little Molly wants to know what dress she'll wear. It will be one of May's cast-offs of course, as they are almost the only clothes the children own. Thank goodness her girls are older than mine otherwise I don't think we would manage, not if we had to buy winter coats and bonnets as well as pretty dresses to wear to a garden party.

Even I will have something new because May gave me a white blouse for my birthday. It has lace at the neck and the cuffs and it will look lovely with my grey skirt. She says it will all be very informal so I don't need to wear a hat. I hope she has told everybody else that.

I must admit I'm excited, and so is Arthur, because the garden party is in honor of Archie's cousin who is visiting from India where he manages a tea plantation. It's not often we have such exotic visitors in Mapleby, so we are looking forward to meeting him. At the moment the only thing anyone in the village is talking about is the garden party and this Mr Robert Parker.

I re-read the entry and then tracked the dates forward. It took quite a while because she hadn't said when the garden party would take place. I found it eventually though, and then my heart almost stopped.

We had such a lovely time. The weather was gloriously sunny but with just the slightest breeze to prevent us from becoming too hot, and the food was marvelous. Not a penny was spared in an attempt to impress Mr. Parker although Arthur says we have to look at it from Archie's point of view. He says that having a large house in Mapleby and a jeweler's shop in town is nothing compared to managing a whole tea plantation, so he's doing all he can to look more prosperous than he really is. I really don't know why he's bothering because he's heaps richer than anyone else in Mapleby. Besides, Mr. Parker doesn't strike me as someone who is impressed by anything unless he chooses to be. He is very handsome though. Tall and dark with the bluest eyes. Even May seems quite smitten and she is the least flirtatious person I know.

There was more further on, a reference to a cricket match where Mr Parker agreed to make up the numbers for Archie's team. The match seemed to be an annual event between the men in the village and Archie's employees, and May always organized the food for afterwards.

The village team won but thanks to Robert, not by much. He made so many runs that at one point we all thought Archie's team would win. Then Jim Oakley from the smithy ran him out and that was that. He was still the hero of the hour though because he saved Archie's team from ignominy. I must say he looked very handsome in his cricketing whites. So dashing that I swear half the village girls are in love with him. He knows it of course; you can see it in the way his eyes twinkle.

I noted that by now all formality had gone and Rose was referring to him as Robert. Then came another another entry, which I wouldn't have been able to decipher if I didn't already know Rose's secret because by then she was writing in a way that hid what she was actually saying.

Arthur has taken the children to see his mother. She hasn't been the same since his father died so he hopes a visit will cheer her up. Joyce was so excited when they set off that I had to tell her to sit still in case she fell off the cart. Molly was a bit tearful because it is the first night she will ever have spent away from home, but when Arthur lifted her up beside him and said she could help him with the horse, her tears dried like magic. I should have gone too but when I said I had a headache Arthur agreed that a rest without the children would do me good. I filled a basket with some of last year's apples that are still good even if they are a bit wrinkly, and picked a big bunch of

129

herbs. I included a cake too. It means we will only have bread and jam for the rest of the week but the smile it brought to Arthur's face was worth it, and it made me feel a bit less guilty.

After I had waved them off and tidied the house, I dressed in my prettiest blouse and walked across the common to the beech wood. When I got there it was as if I had stepped out of time. The sweet perfume of the wild flowers, the murmuring of the insects, the cool green of the glade beneath the beech trees and the puff of cloud drifting across the patch of sky above our heads is something I'll never forget even if I live to be one hundred.

It was Rose's only mistake, that little word '*our*' in the final sentence, but that and the words that followed made it quite clear to me that she and Robert Parker had arranged a tryst far away from prying eyes. She didn't mention him by name but…well you can see for yourself…

I think I went a little bit mad. To have a whole day to myself was such a luxury, and so was the picnic. There were pastries from May's kitchen, and the peaches from Archie's hot house were so ripe that the juice trickled down my chin to where the front of my blouse was undone and I was covered with a warm stickiness that smelled of sunshine. I forgot about time, forgot about Arthur and the children, forgot about all the things I needed to do, and just indulged all my senses.

Until today I didn't know what sun on naked skin felt like. I never imagined a pillow of moss could be so soft either. Lying there was like dying and going to heaven. I abandoned every convention I've ever known and just gave myself up to the moment, and it was delicious.

Of course it came to an end, just as everything comes to an end, but I have the memory. My body has the memory. I will never forget the hardness and the softness, the smells, the murmurings that merged with the birdsong and the bees. I will always remember everything.

The next few words were hidden beneath a blot of ink, which was so unlike Rose that all I could think was that someone had interrupted her until I looked closer and saw that it wasn't a blot at all, but a tearstain. I traced it with my finger, feeling her pain. She knew her life had changed forever but she couldn't explain why, not even in the privacy of her diary, in case someone picked it up and read it.

I closed the notebook and put it at the bottom of the pile because I didn't want anyone else to read it either. Rose's secret was safe with me.

* * *

I didn't sleep much that night. Lying beside Daniel and listening to him breathing I recalled the time we had lain in that very same wood, hidden from the world just like Rose and her lover. It might even have been the same glade and the same mossy bed

Unable to settle, I crept out of bed and tiptoed from the room. Daniel stirred and muttered in his sleep but he didn't wake up, and if he did I knew he was too used to me getting up to see to Leah these days to wonder why my side of the bed was cold. I pushed away memories of the many nights we had slept entwined in each other's arms and went into the kitchen to make a hot drink.

Rose was sitting there, her head on her arms, asleep at the table. Beside her was a half drunk glass of water and she was clutching a balled up handkerchief in one hand. Behind her the fire in the range was banked down for the night so the room was gloomy, with dark shadows in the corners. Clothes were drying on a rack hanging from the ceiling and there was a faint smell of stew, probably the remnants of an evening meal.

I was puzzled. I knew Rose had lived in the cottage as a little girl but what was she doing here now? Surely she and Arthur had a home of their own somewhere in the village, close to his uncle's cobbler's shop. While I was still wondering the door behind me opened and Rose's mother came into the room. She was a lot older than when I had last seen her and her hair was snow white. I knew it was her though because she still looked like Ma. She sounded like her too.

"Rose, lovey, what are you doing here? I thought you went home hours ago."

Raising her head, Rose rubbed her eyes and I was shocked to see how pale and tired she looked. "I can't, Mama. I have to stay until..." she broke into sobs that racked her body.

Her mother's voice was gentle. "It might take days or even weeks, dearie. There's no way of knowing how long."

"How can you be so calm about it? Doesn't it make you angry that he is just lying there and we can't do a thing to help him?"

"Rose, Rose, you mustn't upset yourself like this. It's not your fault he was taken sick when you were walking in the wood to clear your headache. Even if you had been here I doubt it would have made much difference."

"It would have. If I'd visited, like I said I was going to, then I could have helped you carry him to the bed. If I'd been here then you wouldn't have had to leave him lying on the floor all alone while you went for the doctor," Rose's voice was thick with tears of self loathing.

Her mother shook her head. "You really must stop this. The last thing Papa would want is that you make yourself ill over silly regrets. If you want to help him and me then you need to take care of yourself. You need to think of Arthur and the children too. How do you think they feel about their mother being out of the house all the time? Go home, lovey, and get some sleep, and then look after your own family. I'll be fine, especially now Archie sends his groom over every day to check on us."

Reluctantly Rose pushed back her chair and stood up. She was the same height as her mother but much thinner despite the first signs of pregnancy thickening at her waist. With a surge of shock, I noticed she had a few grey hairs at her temple. "I'll only go if you promise to send someone if you need me."

"I promise."

"And you'll let me know what the doctor says. When has Archie arranged for him to call?"

"Tomorrow, although I don't suppose he'll say anything different from all the other times he's called," her mother was ushering her towards the door when there was a cry from the adjoining room. With one accord they turned and ran.

I followed but all I found was my own bedroom with Daniel asleep on his back, snoring gently. Shaken, I climbed back into bed. Rose's beloved Papa was dying and Rose was so full of guilt that he had been taken ill while she was with Robert Parker that she couldn't think straight. How long ago had it happened and had he been bed-ridden ever since? I searched around in my mind for clues and came up with the fact that she was in the early days of her pregnancy, so this had all happened before I saw her in the garden with May. I gave such a heavy sigh that it disturbed Daniel enough to make him turn over and mumble in his sleep. This time travel was beginning to get to me. Not only did I never know when I was going to see Rose, but now her visitations were out of sequence too. For the first time I wondered whether I really should have confided in the vicar so he could visit the cottage and tell her to go away, or did vicars only do that for evil spirits? I sighed again. There was nothing evil about Rose but right at that moment I fervently wished she had never come into my life.

* * *

Daniel and I were just about on speaking terms the following morning. He even ruffled my hair and said he would be home early so to be sure to keep Leah up to see him.

Leah and I waved to him as he drove away and then I forced myself forget Rose and concentrate on my chores until coffee time. Robbie arrived earlier than usual, bringing cakes and a whole lot of information about his great-great-grandfather.

Helping himself to two plates from the cupboard, he placed a cream éclair on each of them and then propped himself against the table. I handed him a mug of coffee and waited. He could barely contain himself.

"My great-great-grandfather was a Robert Parker too, the same as me. Mom emailed me a copy of his letter last night. Look, I've got it here." He held out his cell phone.

I took it and scrolled through the text. By now I was used to the copperplate style of writing that was common when Rose was young, so it didn't take me long to read it. It was from Archie. Robbie watched me, his mouth full of éclair.

Dear Robert

Thank you for your letter. I am so pleased you enjoyed your visit to Mapleby. We certainly loved having you here. The lads in the village are still talking about your success on the cricket pitch and you are young Oliver's hero, something unlikely to change in the near future as I'm afraid I'm a dull old stick compared to you.

You asked me to pass on your good wishes to Rose and May and I have done so. Sadly their father passed away recently. I was able to send my own doctor to attend him and he diagnosed heart failure, probably the result of a bout of rheumatic fever he suffered as a child. His lingering has been distressing for all of us but especially for Rose who has always shared a special rapport with him. His death left her distraught, so much so that May has insisted she and the children stay with us for a while and it seems to be doing the trick. She is smiling again thank goodness, although that could be because she is expecting another child. Both she and Arthur are hoping for a boy this time.

May, as usual, copes with everything. She has also persuaded her mother to spend a few days with us before Rose needs her for her lying in. Once we are sure the baby has arrived safely I am going to take May and the children to the seaside for a few days. I will have some business to attend to while we are there but I daresay they will find plenty to do.

I'm glad you had a safe trip back to India old boy, and that the plantation hadn't suffered too much during your absence. Give my best wishes to that young woman you told me about, and tell her she will be most welcome here at Riverside House when you next return to England, by which time you'll be an old married man. The village girls will be so disappointed to find you no longer a bachelor, and so, I think, will May and Rose.

Ever your affectionate cousin
Archie

Was Oliver Archie's son, and who was the young lady waiting in India for Robert, and did Rose know about her? And would she have cared if she did? There were so many things I wanted to ask but all I managed was, "Where did you mother find the letter?"

"She didn't. One of my cousins found it in some old family papers and sent it to her. She wants me to try to find out who wrote it but it won't be easy because there isn't a surname. Maybe if I ask around someone will remember who lived at a place called Riverside House all those years ago."

I told him because he was bound to find out anyway. "Archie was married to my Great-Great-Aunt May, and the Rose he refers to is my Great-Great-Grandmother."

"You mean the one who nailed the horseshoe to the fence when she was a little girl?"

I nodded. "Yes. May was her sister and she married into money which is why she lived at Riverside House. It was the grand building the council pulled down so the nursing home could be built."

He stared at me. "Really?"

"Yes, really. It's all in Rose's diaries," I lied.

"So your family knew my great-great-grandfather all those years ago, and now here we are. My mother will be thrilled when I tell her." Suddenly a thought struck him. "Is there any chance she could have a look at those diaries, or rather the bits that are about my grandfather's visit?"

"Of course, but she'll have to wait a bit because they are with my Grandma at the moment," I said, glad I had tidied them all into a drawer." There was no way I was letting anyone look at those diaries because if they did they would wonder how I knew so much more than the things that were actually written in them.

Biting into my éclair I deflected his interest away from Rose by asking him what he knew about his great-great-grandfather, Robert Parker. He shrugged.

"I don't know much except that he managed a tea plantation in India. I think he must have been quite young when he died because apparently my great-great-grandmother and their children came back to England alone, and my mother says she married again quite soon afterwards. I think she had three more girls after that."

"How many children did she have with Robert Parker?"

"Two or three, I'm not sure, but one of them must have been a boy because the name was handed down. There's been at least one Robert in every generation of the Parker family for years and years, sometimes more that one."

"You mean you have a cousin called Robert?"

He grinned at me. "No, I have a cousin Bob and a cousin Bobby."

I laughed. "And I thought my family was weird. Bob, Bobby and Robbie. Why don't any of you use Robert?"

"Because that would be my Dad."

I was really laughing now and that was the exact moment that Daniel walked in. He frowned when he saw the empty plates and mugs, and registered the amusement on our faces.

"What are you doing here?" I should have been worried because he never comes home in the middle of the day, but because we were barely back on speaking terms I was too busy feeling resentful to think about anybody else but me.

He gave Robbie a curt nod as he answered. "Your Grandma collapsed this morning. She's in hospital now and your mother is with her but she keeps asking for you. I've come to take you to see her."

I did the one thing I can always be guaranteed to do in an emergency; I panicked. "But Leah hasn't woken up from her morning sleep yet, and when she does she'll need feeding." I could barely hear my protest above the pounding of my heart but I still knew I was being pathetic; I just didn't know how to stop myself. Daniel did though. He took hold of both my hands and made me look at him.

"It's okay, Rachel. We are going to drop Leah off at Rebecca's on the way to the hospital and she will look after her until we get back. All you need to do is pack a bag while I fold up the stroller and put it in the car."

I held onto his hands so tightly that I probably left nail marks. "But what about the shop? Millie finishes at three o'clock."

"All sorted. If I'm late back, then one of her friends will collect the children from school. Your father is going to help out as well."

"Is there anything I can do?" Robbie's voice startled us because we had both forgotten he was there.

"No, but thanks anyway," Daniel shook his head. Taking that as a cue to leave Robbie put Great-Great-Uncle Archie's letter in his pocket and made a hasty exit. I didn't blame him. Up until now he had only seen cheerful, fun-loving Rachel, whereas Daniel was used to the tearful, panic-stricken wreck I turned into the moment there was a crisis.

"Come on, the sooner we arrive at the hospital the better," he gave me a swift hug before going outside to sort out the stroller.

I knew he was right. Grandma, already confused by her dementia, would be totally lost in a big hospital ward, so if she was asking for me then I needed to get there as soon as possible. Keeping that thought in the forefront of my mind

I stuffed nappies, a change of baby clothes and some jars of pureed food into Leah's carry bag, added a tin of formula and some bottles, thankful that I had started to wean her off breast milk, and zipped it up. Then I grabbed my purse, slipped my feet into the sneakers I kept beside the kitchen door, and headed out to the car.

Daniel took Leah's bag from me and put it in the trunk next to the stroller. He frowned when I climbed into the passenger seat though. "Haven't you forgotten something?

I gave him a blank look until it hit me. Leah! I'd forgotten Leah. I burst into tears and I was still crying when he carried her out of the house and strapped her into the baby seat. Once he was sure she was secure he climbed into the driver's seat and pulled me close.

"I'm sure you're not the only mother who has forgotten her baby for a few minutes, Rachel. You would have remembered her before we drove out of the gate."

"But what if I hadn't?" I sobbed into his shoulder. "I don't blame you for not loving me like you used to, not when I'm such a terrible wife and mother."

He drew back and looked at me, frowning again. "What on earth are you talking about?"

"Everything. I'm talking about everything." I couldn't bring myself to say Millie's name but it hung between us, or at least I thought it did, but Daniel refused to engage. Instead he pushed me gently back into the passenger seat and started the engine.

"We'll sort this out later. Right now you need to dry your eyes and make yourself presentable before we reach Rebecca's house."

I knew what he was doing because I had heard that resigned tone of voice a lot when Leah was tiny and he had to cajole me into doing anything other than worry about her. There had even been one week when I refused to have a shower, so frightened was I that something would happen while I was away. I had only really started to get better when everyone had stopped fussing and Daniel had started to tell me what to do. Somehow that had put me back on track. I don't know if Doctor Gove told him to do it or whether my irrational behavior drove him to it, but it had worked, and from then on I had been more or less fine.

It worked now too, and by the time my sister lifted Leah from the car I was back to my normal self. I had even managed to tidy my hair and put on some lip gloss in the short time it took us to drive to her house. Although she looked worried, she smiled at me.

"I don't know what it is between you and Grandma but if anyone can help her, it's you Rachel. Now off you go and don't think about Leah. You know how much I enjoy looking after her, and the boys will love to see her when they come home from school."

Chapter Fourteen

We were almost at the hospital when the thought struck me. "Why did Ma call you instead of me?"

Daniel glanced at me. "She did call you, several times, but your cell phone went to voice mail. She texted you too."

I rummaged in my purse for my cell phone. It was set on silent. I had forgotten to turn the sound on when I woke up so had spent the entire morning cut off from the world. I had been laughing and flirting with Robbie and eating cream cakes while Grandma was suffering in hospital and Ma was trying to contact me. I went cold inside. What if it had been worse? What if something had happened to Daniel and nobody could get me? What if he had had a heart attack just like Rose's father and nobody could find me to tell me about it until it was too late. For one panic-stricken moment I forgot about cars and ambulances and all the safety nets of modern life and imagined I lived like Rose.

Daniel saw the expression on my face and shook his head. "It didn't happen, Rachel. Whatever you are worrying about, it didn't happen."

"No, but it might have done, and then I would have been almost as guilty as Rose," I whispered, but he was too busy looking for a space to park the car to hear me.

* * *

Grandma was as pale as the pillow behind her head and Ma didn't look much better. They smiled when Daniel and I walked up to the bed though, Ma with relief and Grandma with satisfaction.

"Rose said you'd both come," she told me, and then closed her eyes.

I shrugged when Ma raised her eyebrows, and for once I wasn't lying. I had no idea what Rose had told Grandma. I didn't find out for ages either because she wasn't talking. Ma looked at her inert figure in consternation.

"She seems to have worn herself out calling for you."

I took hold of one of Grandma's hands. It was warm and I felt a faint pressure as her fingers curled in mine. She wasn't asleep, she was just biding her time. I settled down to wait.

Ma stayed in the chair opposite and Daniel set off in search of coffee. When he returned with three cardboard cups of questionable liquid he suggested Ma take a break once she had finished hers. "I passed the hospital canteen on my way back to the ward and lunch smells good," he said.

I saw my chance. "Why don't you both go? You haven't had a thing since early this morning Daniel, and Ma would probably appreciate the company. I'll be fine here with Grandma until you get back."

They both looked doubtful, Daniel because he had seen how panicked I was earlier, and Ma because she was worried. "I wish we had never shown her a single photo, let alone tried to persuade her to remember the past. She's done nothing but talk about Granny Rose ever since she saw that picture of her. On her worst days she even confuses her with you, Rachel, so who knows what she'll say when she wakes up and sees you next to the bed."

I aimed for a suitably understanding expression as I nodded my agreement because I knew that if I didn't Ma wouldn't leave me on my own with Grandma. "It's only because I look a bit like Rose," I said, as I wondered how long it would be before Ma and Daniel totally trusted my sanity again. Then I remembered all the times I had seen Rose and spoken to her and I didn't blame them because I wasn't entirely sure how sane I was myself anymore.

"I suppose so," Ma looked doubtful. She didn't demur when Daniel asked her a second time though. Draining her coffee cup, she stood up and stretched. Then she picked up the large tote bag she carries with her everywhere and followed him out of the ward. Left to my own devices but aware that we didn't have that much time, I squeezed Grandma's hand.

"You can open your eyes now because they've gone."

She peered at me through two slits. I laughed. "Did Rose put you up to this?"

"Rose wanted Daniel, too."

"You mean she wanted me to realize how much I need Daniel and this was the only way she could think to arrange it. I suppose she was the one who made me forget to switch on my cell phone this morning too." I was getting better at reading Rose's mind by the minute. I was also beginning to have an inkling about what she was up to.

Grandma nodded. "She made me promise."

I frowned. "Well, from now on you can tell her to leave you out of it. If she wants to talk to me she knows where I live."

But Grandma was too intent on relaying the rest of her message to listen. "Daniel is a good man."

"I know he is, and so was Arthur. Tell Rose I know she loved Arthur. Tell her I understand."

* * *

We stayed long enough for the duty doctor to check Grandma out again and discharge her back to the nursing home. When Ma wondered why he wasn't keeping her in overnight for observation, he shook his head and said she would sleep better in her own bed. He assured us she had suffered no ill effects from her seizure at the same time that he confessed to being puzzled as to what exactly had been wrong with her. He then told Ma to ask the staff at the nursing home to keep a close eye on her, patted Grandma's hand, and walked briskly down the ward to his next, far more deserving patient.

Daniel helped Grandma into a wheelchair and pushed her down the long corridor to the hospital entrance while Ma and I followed on behind, Ma muttering about time wasted, and me keeping quiet.

It wasn't until after she was tucked up in bed in the nursing home that Daniel asked me what Grandma had said. I shrugged.

"Not much. She just talked a bit about Rose and then closed her eyes again."

I could tell he didn't believe me. He knew I had a secret but he wasn't going to ask, the same as he wouldn't ask me about my mid-morning coffee break with Robbie. It was one of the things I had always liked best about him, the respect he had for other people's privacy. I wished I could be as understanding but I knew I couldn't, especially as far as Millie Carter was concerned. Rose might have taught me not to play with fire but she hadn't taught me tolerance or how to curb my temper. I had to do all that on my own.

* * *

We were back in the car together and on our way to Rebecca's to pick up Leah when Daniel pulled into a quiet layby and killed the engine. I stared at him. "What are you doing?"

"This," he said, and slipped him arm around my shoulders, pulled me to him and, tilting my lips to his, kissed me very slowly and very thoroughly. When we finally drew apart my pulse was racing and when I saw the expression in his eyes my breath caught in my throat. For a moment I thought he might throw caution to the wind and make love to me right there, in full view of passing traffic. He didn't though. Instead he grinned at me as he started the engine again.

"That's so you know how much I love you, but I think I'd better keep both hands occupied until we get home."

I laughed. Had Rose manipulated the day's events just for this? If she had, then I wasn't complaining. How could I have been so stupid as to think there was anything going on between Daniel and Millie when he still wanted to kiss me like that? Besides, when would they have the time or opportunity? I had more chance of an affair with Robbie what with Leah being asleep during the day and nobody else being around. I blocked out the fact that Millie would probably be living over the shop by the end of the week.

* * *

Rose didn't get things all her own way though. Firstly, Rebecca insisted we stay for a meal, and while we were eating it, Ma arrived. She wasn't in the best of moods thanks to spending most of the day at the hospital and the fact that Pa was too worn out from his stint at the shop to take her to their weekly quiz night.

"Why don't you go on your own?" Rebecca asked.

"Because I'm shattered, too," Ma snapped. Then she turned on me. "Was it my imagination or did Grandma pull some sort of stunt?"

I feigned total innocence. "She's ninety-four years old Ma. Long past pulling stunts."

"You don't know my mother," she muttered. "Dementia or not she's up to something and I want to know what it is. What did she say to you Rachel, because she's refusing to talk to me?"

My hands were hidden in my lap so I crossed my fingers. "Nothing much, she just rambled on about Rose as usual."

Daniel saw my crossed fingers and cut across Ma's next outburst. "She just keeps confusing Rose with Rachel."

"Well it's got to stop. You need to visit her again and talk about what's happening in the here and now instead of

144

showing her all those pictures and pretending you know what she's talking about."

Swallowing my indignation that it was Ma herself who had started the whole thing by digging out the box of photos in the first place, I nodded. "I'll do my best but she might forget."

"Not if we both go she won't. I'll meet you there later on this week

"I'll come too if you like," Rebecca offered. Then she laughed. "You have to give it to Grandma. She still knows how to keep us all dancing attendance even at ninety-four."

Ma wasn't amused and I didn't blame her because she was the one who the nurses called whenever anything went wrong. "Don't worry," I said. "I'll find a way to stop her thinking about Rose."

* * *

"Don't you want to know what she said?" I asked. I was sitting on Daniel's lap and we were sharing a glass of wine. Leah was in bed asleep, the house was quiet, and we were tormenting ourselves by delaying returning to the passion we had shared in the car.

"Only if you want to tell me," he ran his hand along the length of my leg, raising goose bumps.

"I don't really…well it's more I can't because it's not my secret, which is why I didn't say anything to Ma."

"Then don't say anything to me either because I can think of something I'd far rather do," he put the glass of wine down and turned his attention to the front of my blouse.

"And you don't mind?"

"I don't mind, especially not now, not at this very minute." My blouse undone he was liberating me from my less than attractive nursing bra when his cell phone rang. Ignoring it, he captured my breasts, and within seconds I was moaning with a pent up desire that spilled over as one

145

of his hands dipped lower, breaching the waistband of my jeans.

"Later," he murmured as I twisted towards him and grabbed his T-shirt. "This is for you." And then he tipped me off his lap and onto the couch, removed the rest of my clothes and proved very conclusively that he meant what he said.

The phone rang again and then again and we still ignored it, too intent on repairing all the hurt we had inflicted on one another in recent months to let the outside world in. It wasn't until it rang for a fourth time that Daniel reached out and answered it, his voice languid with the aftermath of sex. While he listened, I walked my fingers across his chest and then curled them into the whorls of golden hair that gradually tapered to a V just where his belt would have been if he had still been wearing one. It was only when Daniel tensed and then swung his legs to the floor and sat up that I realized it was something serious. I tuned in to what he was saying.

"I'll come straight away. No, don't touch anything thing until I get there."

I sat up too, the warm fuzziness that had enveloped me fading fast. "What is it?"

"Someone's put a brick through the shop window."

I stared at him. "Who on earth would do a thing like that?"

"Kids probably. I don't know. I'll have to go and sort it out though, board it up or something. Millie's called the police but it will be ages before they get here now the local police station has closed."

I wasn't interested in the politics of local policing, however. As far as I was concerned Millie's involvement was of far more importance. "Was that her on the phone?"

He nodded, halfway into his jeans. "I meant to say. She and the children are sleeping over the shop at the moment."

I remembered what Robbie had told me. "But the bathroom still needs fixing and the decorating isn't finished."

146

"I see Robbie's been keeping you up to date," he said, pulling his T-shirt over his head.

"Which is more than you have." Despite what had just happened between us, I could feel my temper building. How dare Daniel move Millie into the shop without telling me?

He shook his head as he bent to tie his shoelaces. "It's not what you think, Rachel. The person who lives in the room above her in that god awful place she's in at the moment let his bath overflow, and the water flooded her bedroom. I said she and the boys could sleep above the shop until it's sorted. She still goes home first thing every morning and cooks all her meals there."

I should have felt sorry for Millie, but instead I just added her latest misfortune to the long list of things I held against her. "You have no idea what I think," I said. "No idea at all."

He picked up his keys and made for the door. As he opened it he turned to look at me. "That's where you're wrong. I do know what you're thinking, quite a lot of the time, and right at this minute I don't like it at all."

He didn't slam the door or do anything else inflammatory but I still hurled a cushion across the room. Pathetic, I know. Something hard, something that I could have broken would have been so much more satisfying. Feeling beyond miserable I tossed my discarded clothes into the wash basket and went into the bedroom to fetch my pajamas. Then I tiptoed into the nursery to check on Leah. Rose was waiting for me. She looked terrible and I had a horrible feeling that it was my fault. I hardened my heart.

"Stop interfering," I said. "And leave my grandmother out of it as well. She's a very old lady, far too frail to play your games for you."

Rose just looked at me, her eyes rimmed red from what...exhaustion or tears. I sighed. "It would be much easier if you just told me what you want. All this cloak and dagger stuff is getting me down."

To my surprise she gestured towards the door. I followed her through to the kitchen and when she was sure I was watching, she pointed to the kitchen drawer. I opened it and piled the notebooks onto the table.

Communicating more directly than she ever had before, she indicated that I should spread them out on the table. I did as she asked and then watched her bend to read the dates on the front of each one. She had to squint her eyes to do so and for some reason it amused me to see that, ghost or no, she needed spectacles. When she looked up she saw me smiling and for a fleeting moment she smiled too. It transformed her face back into that of the young Rose, the girl without a care in the world, The girl who, like me, was loved by everyone but hadn't known how lucky she was until she almost destroyed it.

I don't know where those thoughts came from...Rose probably...and they were in and out of my head before I had time to grasp them. A shadowy memory lingered though and when our eyes met I was sure Rose had planted it there.

Then her smile faded and as it did the color of her hair faded too, and her face lost its bloom. Before my eyes she turned into an old woman as her lovely dark hair whitened, wrinkles formed around her eyes, and sharp lines curved around her mouth in a parenthesis. Her hands aged too. As she pointed to one of the notebooks I saw they were veined and thin, and rough from hard work. Instead of being scared I wanted to cry.

"You want me to read this one?" I picked up the notebook and looked at the date on the cover. 1902. When I turned back Rose had gone.

Chapter Fifteen

With nothing else to do and not wanting to think about what Daniel had said, I opened the diary, wondering why Rose wanted me to read it. The first couple of pages were just a litany of complaints about household chores and the frustrations of looking after small children when the weather was wet and the garden was muddy. Then it segued into something much darker as she poured out her feelings about Arthur.

She begrudged the money he gave his unmarried sisters, she resented the time he spent working for what she considered a pittance, she was angry when he patched up shoes for nothing if a villager didn't have the money to pay him or, almost as bad in her eyes, accepted payment in vegetables or, on one occasion, much to her disgust, with a basket of windfall apples. According to Rose, Arthur was weak, a poor provider, and an even poorer businessman, and she couldn't understand why everyone loved him. It was this more than anything that seemed to occupy her thoughts.

Even little Robert loves him best. I spend all day cleaning the house, washing the clothes, caring for the children and cooking the meals, and then Arthur walks through the door and they all run to him for cuddles and games. He encourages it with his smiles and silly songs, and if the weather is good he will play with them in the garden or take them across the fields to search for beech nuts or mushrooms or wild strawberries...whatever is in season, and they always come back with something. They always behave better with him too and sometimes, when I see them all snuggled up together in bed while Arthur tells them a story, I just can't bear it.

Later, when they are asleep, he comes and sits with me, and when we are in bed he tells me how much he loves me, but I just say I'm too tired and turn my back and after a moment he sighs and then we are silent. We lie side-by-side, each pretending we are asleep, but both knowing we are wide awake and staring into the darkness.

Sometimes I wish Arthur would shout at me instead of being so nice all the time, but he never does. Instead he brings me wild flowers from the fields and makes me beautiful shoes from the softest leather, while I carry on being bad tempered and mean to him. Inside though, I know he wants to shake some sense into me, he wants to tell me to pull myself together, he wants me to be the Rose I was when we were first married, and I want to be that person too but....

I stopped reading and snapped the notebook shut because Arthur was a bit too much like Daniel for my liking, and although it pained me to admit it, Rose and I had far more in common than our looks. I was still sitting on the couch with the notebook on my lap when the light dimmed around me and without any sense of disorientation I suddenly found myself sitting beside a crackling fire in an unfamiliar room. Rose sat opposite me. Old and wrinkled and with thinning white hair, she seemed shrunken. She was darning a sock and there was a sewing basket beside her chair. As I watched she glanced at the clock on the mantle and a moment later I heard an outer door open.

Although I knew the man who came into the room was Arthur I didn't recognize him because he had changed so much. The dashing mustache had gone, and so had his hair. He looked smaller too, and very weary. His smile was the same though and it lit up his face as Rose put down her sewing and got up to greet him.

"How have you been today?" he asked as he unwound a long scarf from his neck and took off his coat.

Rose gave the slightest of shrugs as they both went through to the kitchen where she busied herself making tea.

I followed of course and as she reached up into a cupboard for a tea caddy I saw the growth at her throat. It was large and smooth and I knew what it was because Ma had talked about it when she first saw the photos of Rose. It was a goiter, a growth on Rose's thyroid gland. Now I understood why she had a shawl draped around her shoulders. It was so she could hide her neck if somebody came to call.

Arthur didn't appear to mind it when hugged her close and gave her a kiss though. Remembering what she had written in her diary, I held my breath. I didn't think I would be able to bear it if she pushed him away. She didn't. Instead she returned his kiss with enthusiasm and told him to sit at the table.

"Supper is almost ready," she said. Her voice was reedy and strained and I guessed it was because of the goiter.

I sat at the table too and listened while Arthur told her about his day. Then, after he'd eaten his last mouthful, he began to clear the table. When Rose began to help him he gently pushed her back into her chair.

"I'll do it. You know how breathless you get."

So Rose sat and watched him wash the dishes and I sat and watched them both. I was still watching them when Rose began to talk.

"Molly called in today. She told me such funny stories about the children in her class."

Arthur smiled over the soap suds. "Two daughters who are school teachers and a son who is training to be a doctor. What did we do to produce such a clever family?"

"We were sensible enough to have wealthy in-laws who were prepared to support them while they were training," Rose replied with some of her old tartness, but her heart wasn't really in it, and Arthur knew it. He nodded.

"We owe Archie and May a great deal but you had something to do with it as well, my love. If you hadn't read to them so often or pushed them to be the best they could be, then they might have turned out very differently."

Tears clotted Rose's eyelashes as she replied. "You gave them something far more important than I did. You gave them unconditional love the same as my parents gave me.

Why couldn't I do that, Arthur? Why did I always want more from them… from you?"

I saw from the expression on her face that she hadn't meant to to say the last bit and would have taken it back if she could. For a long moment the steady drip from one of the taps was the only sound in the room, then Arthur carried on washing the dishes and we all breathed again. I thought that was the end of their conversation but it wasn't. Neither of them said another word until Arthur had put the last dish away. Then he dried his hands and came across the kitchen to where she was sitting.

"It wasn't really the children or me that were the problem, Rose. You wanted more from life. That's why you pushed us all. You wanted Joyce and Molly to escape the drudgery of your everyday existence, and you wanted Robert to earn a lot more than me. You fought hard to make sure they had the choices we never had."

She stared at him. "I didn't realize you understood."

"Of course I did. I always understood, but I was afraid that if I said anything our life would change. I was always afraid of losing you."

Her smile was so sad when she answered that I felt tears sting my own eyes. "I always loved you, even when I was angry."

"I was too much of a coward to test it."

With something between a sigh and a moan, Rose stood up and held out her hand. "Let's go through and sit beside the fire so you can rest."

I followed as they walked, hand in hand, back to their small sitting room, and then watched from a shadowy corner as Arthur lowered himself into the chair Rose had been sitting on when I first saw her. To my amazement he then pulled her down with him until she was sitting on his lap. It took them a few moments to get comfortable and by the time she was snuggled into his chest they were both laughing.

"I can't imagine why you want an old bag of bones like me sitting on your lap when you know you'll have cramp in your legs in less than five minutes." Rose giggled, sounding more like the girl she once had been.

He turned his head and kissed her. "You'll never be old to me."

"In that case you need new spectacles," she said. Then, after a moment's silence, she picked up the conversation they had been having in the kitchen. "You were never a coward, Arthur. You are the backbone of this family, the one who always holds us together when things go wrong and who makes me feel blessed every single day. You have always let me and the children be ourselves, even though I know we've grieved you at times. And you always love us totally and unconditionally, even when we are our very worst selves."

Although Rose was talking about the whole family I knew she was really talking about herself. I knew Arthur did too, but his reply still startled me.

"I knew I was going to be a cobbler from as far back as I can remember, and I never resented it because when we were young that's just how things were. All boys followed their father's trade if they were lucky enough to have one. Mending shoes wasn't what I wanted for Robert though, and I wanted more for the girls too, and for you. It's the reason I never minded when you stayed with May and Archie, because I knew you needed a different conversation as well as time away from the grind of putting endless meals on the table. It used to frighten me though because whenever we were at Riverside House you were always so full of confidence and looked so lovely that I couldn't quite believe you belonged to me."

"I only looked lovely because I was dressed in May's castoffs. It's amazing what a pretty dress and hat can do." There was no bitterness in Rose's voice when she answered him, just an acceptance of the past.

He smiled as he continued. "I'll never forget that picnic down by the river. Do you remember? It was when Archie's cousin was visiting from India. What was his name?"

"Robert." Rose didn't flinch.

"Oh, of course. I should have remembered because you liked the name so much you chose it for our son."

Rose stayed silent, but from where I was standing I could see the color had drained from her cheeks. Arthur continued, oblivious.

"It was one of those days that stick in the mind. Glorious weather and everyone so happy. And you were on top form, the life and soul of the party, making everyone laugh and persuading them to play silly games. I was so proud of you, but I was scared too, because when I saw the admiration in everyone's eyes I realized how much more potential you had than me. It was then that I realized how, eventually, our life here in Mapleby would cripple you."

She shifted slightly on his lap but she didn't look at him. Instead she answered in a halting voice that could have been the result of her damaged vocal chords, but which I knew was actually her conscience. "I remember that day too, and I remember wishing we could always live like that. It took me a long time to realize how stupid I was being. Nobody lives like that, not even if they have a lot of money. Life intervenes. May, for all her wealth, wasn't really happy with Archie you know. How could she be when he mostly ignored her? Eventually I understood that we all have to do things we don't want to do just to survive, and all the time I was working that out, you just loved me. I wish I hadn't wasted so much time being angry, Arthur."

It was as if she was putting all my thoughts into words but with the wisdom of old age. How long would it have taken me to realize how lucky I was if Rose hadn't shown me? Suddenly I wanted to get back to my own life so I could tell Daniel how much I loved him. If I didn't he really might start wanting Millie Carter with her long red hair and spectacular figure. It seemed as if the force of my longing made me wake up at that moment, but actually it was Daniel gently shaking me, "Come on, sleepyhead, it's time for bed."

* * *

I stirred, my eyes blurry as I tried to reorientate myself back into our own sitting room. Beside me, Daniel flopped down onto the sofa, his face slack with weariness.

"Was anything stolen?" I suddenly remembered where he had been and what had happened.

He shook his head. "No, it was just a smashed window, but there was glass everywhere so we had to dismantle the display. Luckily Robbie Parker turned up and helped too or it would have taken a lot longer. He was on his way home from the pub when he saw what had happened, so he fetched some wood and made it secure for me."

"That was kind of him." For once my heart didn't flip over at the sound of Robbie's name. It was if he was talking about a stranger. I then said the most surprising thing. "And is Millie okay? It must have been very scary for her and the children."

He glanced at me, saw my concern was genuine, and smiled. "She's fine. Millie's made of tough stuff but I guess she's had to be."

I swallowed, knowing I had to apologize. "I'm sorry I was so horrible, Daniel. I don't know what gets into me sometimes. Tell me you forgive me."

He gave me a hug. "Nothing to forgive."

"But there is, you know there is. I spend most of my time being mean about Millie Carter and cranky with you. How you put up with me I can't imagine."

"Mmm, maybe it's because I love you," he said, kissing my temple.

"And I love you," I whispered, turning towards him and sliding both my arms around his neck. We stayed there for a long time, with me holding him so tightly that eventually he had to break away to breathe.

"I know you do," he said. "And I also know you need more to occupy you so I've come up with a plan."

I leaned back slightly so I could read his face. He smiled but his smile was tinged with doubt. "Don't get angry until you've heard me out."

Given that I had just apologized for being angry all the time, I guess he thought it was a good moment to test me out. I waited.

"Millie and I were talking while we were clearing up and I sort of said you've been a bit scratchy since Leah was born."

I waited some more, keeping a lid on my feelings even though the thought of him discussing me with Millie made me want to scream. He ploughed on, not at all sure how I was going to react.

"Millie says you need something to do other than just look after Leah. She says she was the same when her first was born, but when she suggested taking a part time job her husband became really angry."

"And we all know how that ended." I kept the sarcasm out of my voice with an effort.

He nodded. "Yes, but it made me think, and when I remembered how good you were with the customers, and how you were always the one with the best ideas about growing the business, I knew she was right. You were the one who said we had to start stocking freshly made sandwiches and pies for the local workers to buy at lunchtime, and we wouldn't have set up the deli counter unless you had insisted either, so I made a suggestion to Millie and she's all for it if you are."

I was almost out of patient waiting but I kept my tongue clamped between my teeth while he finished.

"How about you take over from Millie when she goes to fetch her boys from school, and do the last three hours each day while she gives Leah her tea?"

I stared at him. Was he out of his mind? Did he really expect me to hand Leah over to Millie Carter the thief, the woman who had been homeless until he offered her the rooms over the shop without any sort of a by-your-leave from me? Then it began to sink in. Leah would be upstairs while I was working so if there was any sort of a problem Millie and I could swop places, plus I was bored and I knew it. I missed the everyday contact with other people, I missed making business decisions, I missed knowing what was going on. My final thought clinched it. If I was right there, in the shop, Millie Carter wouldn't stand a chance of getting her claws into my husband.

Daniel waited while the thoughts swirled around my head and the relief on his face when I nodded almost made me laugh. Instead, I took the upper hand. Daniel and Millie Carter might have come up with a pretty wonderful idea but I wasn't about to let them dictate exactly how it would work.

"When does Millie move into the shop?"

"The weekend after next I think. Ask Robbie when he's here tomorrow. He'll know when the bathroom will be finished."

I nodded, wondering how much it had taken him to say that considering how he had walked in on our little tete-a-tete over coffee and éclairs earlier that day. I didn't let it stop me setting the pace though.

"I will, and as soon as I know I'll talk to Millie about a trial run."

* * *

We were in bed less than ten minutes later, and five minutes after that Daniel was asleep. I lay awake for a long time though and thought of all that had happened during the day, and when I finally drifted off to sleep I heard Rose's last words in my dreams.

I wish I hadn't wasted so much time being angry, Arthur.

157

Chapter Sixteen

By the time Robbie arrived for coffee the following day I had rationalized the guilt I felt at not finding Leah enough to keep me stimulated, and was already making plans. He sensed the difference as soon as he stepped into the kitchen and deposited a paper bag containing two currant buns onto the table.

"You look full of the joys of spring. Has something happened?"

"Yes, I'm about to become a working woman again."

He listened while I explained and then shrugged when I very belatedly thanked him for securing the shop window the previous evening. "I had the wood and the tools, so it didn't take very long. Besides, I had nothing else to do."

I nodded and then prattled on about the benefits of my new life and how seeing Millie's boys every day would be good for Leah too. It took me a while but eventually I realized that his heart wasn't in it so I stopped wittering and asked him what was wrong.

He shrugged again. "Nothing much. Just someone I was hoping to see has sent word she's cancelling her visit to Mapleby yet again."

"A girl?" I was jolted right out of my self absorption.

When he nodded I wondered why I had ever thought there was a chance of anything developing between us given that I was married with a baby and he was more than a bit of a hunk. Someone who looked like Robbie probably left a string of girls behind whenever he signed yet another building contract and moved to yet another town. I tried to remember where he had been working immediately before he came to Mapleby and realized I had never been interested enough to find out. Ashamed, I put my own problems to one side and asked him.

He stared morosely into this coffee mug, swirling the dark liquid to and fro. "London, and before that Spain and before that the Caribbean. I could go on but you'd be bored."

Something clicked in my mind and before I could stop myself I blurted it out. "You came here to find Ella, didn't you?"

He sighed. "Is it really that obvious? Yes, I'm here for Ella. I thought she would come to Mapleby to see her Dad, and that when she did I could put things right between us. It wasn't until I talked to you that day at the pub that I realized she has more or less given up on him, too, although with less reason as far as I can see. I'm nothing if not an optimist though, so I've taken to eating there most evenings just in case she turns up, so when Tom told me she was visiting next weekend I started to prepare myself for the confrontation we are bound to have. Then, yesterday, he told me she's cancelled again. That's how I know she isn't coming. He's really cut up about it you know, mostly because he has no idea why she's stopped coming to Mapleby. I feel much the same and I guess you do too."

Remembering how close Ella and I had been as children, and then as teenagers, I felt a pang of guilt. I'd let her down the same as I'd let Daniel down. Every time I sent her an email or a text message, it was all about me. I never asked her about her life, never asked her why she didn't come home. I just assumed it was because Mapleby was boring compared to her new life, and that I was boring as well. I had chosen to feel neglected instead of worried. One glance at Robbie's miserable face made me decide it was time I started to think about other people again.

"When did you last see her?" I asked.

"In London when I asked her to marry me."

"I suppose she turned you down?"

He shook his head. "Not exactly, she just put on her coat and called a taxi. It took her straight to the airport and the next thing I knew she was working on a film set in Monaco."

"So what did you do?"

"I fired off a whole string of angry voice messages that I regretted as soon as I pressed send."

I felt his pain because I knew how easily I could have done the same to Daniel. Hesitating, I chose my next words carefully. "Am I right in thinking that you still want to marry her?"

He nodded. "More than anything, but I can see it won't work. Ella is already married to her job. I faced up to that when she ignored my messages and then blocked my phone calls. Not that I really blame her because I said some pretty hurtful things, things that I want to take back, which is why I looked for a job in Mapleby."

"So finding out that one of your ancestors has connections with the village is pure coincidence?"

He nodded again. "It's made the waiting more bearable though, and you have too, Rachel. Your friendship means more than you'll ever know. Without you my life in Mapleby would be very bleak indeed."

"So I just imagined you were flirting with me, did I?" I couldn't keep the chagrin out of my voice.

He grinned, and suddenly he was sexy Robbie again. "Not entirely, because you are very pretty and old habits die hard."

I gave him a despairing look. "You might enjoy flirting, Robbie Parker, but one day it will get you into serious trouble. And another thing, why didn't you tell me about Ella as soon as you realized who I was. That day in the pub when you learned I was Rachel Pavalak, the friend she often talked about, you almost said something didn't you?"

"Yes, but then Daniel said you had more or less lost touch, so I changed my mind. Besides, it didn't seem right to open up to strangers."

"Well I'm not a stranger any more am I, so tell me what to do and I'll do it. I want to see Ella almost as much as you do, and her Dad needs to see her more than both of us."

* * *

160

I spent the rest of the day planning and by the time Daniel arrived home I knew what I was doing for the rest of the week. First though, I had to share it all. I was never going to keep anything from him ever again, except for Rose. I was never going to tell anyone about Rose.

After he had tucked Leah into bed and we had eaten our supper, I led him out into the garden, and while we rocked side-by-side on the double swing he had fixed up when we first bought the cottage, I told him almost everything I knew about my family, the history of the nursing home, and Robbie's relationship with Ella. By the time I finished he was totally bemused.

"Why didn't you tell me all this earlier?"

"Because I was too busy being angry," I said. "Besides I've only just begun to piece everything together, and Robbie didn't tell me about Ella, I guessed."

"But what about his connection with your family?"

"That came out of the blue when his mother discovered where he was working."

"So now I suppose you want to get him and Ella back together."

I nodded. "I don't know how, though. I could start bombarding Ella with messages but if I did she would probably guess I had an ulterior motive after such a long silence."

"Maybe you could tell her Tom is ill."

I looked at him in alarm. "He isn't, is he?"

"Not so you'd notice because he never complains, but his arthritis is so bad now that he can't change the barrels on the beer pumps any more. I've done a few for him, and so have his other regulars, but soon he'll have to employ a full time barman to help him."

A memory of Rose's thin hands sprang to my mind, along with the painful nodules on Arthur's fingers, which I'd barely noticed at the time but which had somehow become part of my memory. They had had their love to sustain them though, despite Rose's best attempts at destroying it,

161

whereas Tom had nothing. I was suddenly filled with determination.

"In that case it's about time she learned a few home truths."

* * *

I sent Ella an email the following morning. I made it as casual as possible, filling it with news about Leah and bringing her up to date with village gossip. I even told her about my plan to go back to work part time. I didn't mention Tom until the end and even then I kept it light, merely remarking on the fact that he now had to rely on his customers to keep the beer barrels full. I didn't mention Robbie either. I just told her that a builder was renovating the house next to our cottage.

Then I called Ma and told her I was coming to lunch. I wasn't sure how pleased she would be to see me given our brief contretemps about Grandma, so I didn't give her an option. She sounded fine about it though, and when Leah and I arrived, hot from our long trek up the dusty path leading to the farm, the table was laid and there was an appetizing aroma coming from a pan on the hob.

"It's only soup," she said. "But you can fill up with cheese if it's not enough."

I kissed her, handed Leah over to Pa, who doted on her more than the rest of his grandchildren put together although he tried very hard not to show it, and sat down with a sigh of relief. During lunch we chatted about mundane things while Leah, able to sit up now as long as she had the security of a cushion behind her, amused herself playing with a set of brightly colored plastic beakers. I didn't introduce the real reason for my visit until we had finished eating and Ma was brewing a pot of tea.

"Have you ever heard of the Trayner family?" I asked, ever so casually.

Ma didn't even turn around. "They're Grandma's distant relatives. I think the connection is through your Great-Great-Aunt May, Granny Rose's sister. I thought you were supposed to be the expert on family history nowadays Rachel, not me."

I defended myself even though I didn't actually care. "Although I've managed to find out quite a lot from Rose's diaries and the photos, it's difficult to get further without surnames."

"I suppose so," she pushed a mug of tea across the table towards me and lowered herself into a chair on the opposite side of the table, her face creased with the effort of remembering. "I can remember Grandma saying that May had a little girl very late in her married life when her other children were almost grown. Her name was Sarah and I'm sure she married someone called Matthew Trayner. She inherited Riverside House when May and her husband died because by then she was the only one left. Both her older sisters succumbed to the 1918 influenza epidemic, and her brothers were killed during the Great War."

An unexpected coldness seeped through me despite the summer heat. It was followed by a feeling of deep shame. The complaints I had about my own life were nothing compared to something so terrible. "I didn't know."

Ma shrugged. "No reason why you should because it was all a very long time ago. As far as I can remember, Sarah and her husband lived at Riverside until their children grew up, and then they upped sticks and moved to London."

"And sold the estate to the council, who eventually sold it to Southern Care Homes Limited, who demolished it and built the nursing home Grandma is in."

She narrowed her eyes. "So you worked that out, then?"

"Only because one of the nurses told me that an old Mr. Trayner once owned the land the nursing home is on now. I had no idea we were related to him." I certainly wasn't going to tell her I had seen May and Rose in the garden with their children. The thought prompted another question, though.

"What about Rose's children? Did they all survive the war?"

"As far as I know they did. Robert, her son, was training to be a doctor when it started and he went to the front as soon as he qualified and spent two years patching up the wounded, poor devil, but he survived. Her daughters survived too. Molly, who was Grandma's mother, married her sweetheart as soon as he came home from the front, but Joyce remained a spinster because there weren't enough men to go around by the end of the war."

I hid the relief I felt that at least Rose and Arthur had been spared the grief of losing a child by asking another question. "And what about Robert's children? I know Molly was Grandma's mother, but what about Robert? Did he marry and have a family too?"

For a moment Ma looked blank then she remembered. "Yes, he did. He married someone called….um…Celia, that's it. Celia. She came from somewhere near Devon so he bought into a practice down there and spent the rest of his life as a country doctor."

"And did he visit Granny Rose? Did he keep in touch with her?"

She stared at me. "Why ever wouldn't he? Of course he kept in touch and his children did too. Grandma played with them when she was small. I remember her telling me how excited she was whenever her cousins visited from Devon, not that either of us are going to remind her about it now. Do you hear me, Rachel? I don't want you to say another word to her about Rose ever again."

I took no notice of course. How could I when I still had to unravel the complications of our family even if I never told a soul about my findings.

* * *

I was up bright and early the next morning and the first thing I did was look at my cell phone. I wasn't really surprised there was nothing from Ella. It was early days. I was still disappointed though, but I didn't say a word to Robbie when he arrived in time for coffee. Instead I filled his mug and told him I was going to make a batch of chocolate chip cookies later on, so not to bring any cakes tomorrow.

"Whatever will you do when next door is finished and there's no one to have coffee with?" he teased.

"I'll make friends with my new neighbors," I told him. Then I explained the family connection to the Trayners.

* * *

I was on my way to the nursing home to see Grandma when he called out to me from the house next door. It was a hive of industry by now, with workmen coming and going, and trucks churning up the grass verge beside the house as bricks and cement were delivered. I waved to him, thinking he was just saying hello, but when he waved his arms more frantically I realized he wanted me to stop.

We met at the garden gate and after he had made a fuss of Leah, who now appeared to regard him as one of the family, he turned to me with a smile. "I thought you'd like to know that the Trayners are flying in from the States on Thursday and travelling down to Mapleby at the weekend."

I felt a burst of excitement. Something was happening. I know it sounds fanciful but I could feel it in the air and it filled me with so much energy that I arrived at the nursing home forty minutes before Ma was due instead of the half-an-hour I had allowed myself.

Grandma was sitting in her usual chair by the window. I went and found a nurse and asked if it would be okay to take her outside for a while. She nodded. "Wait a moment and I'll get someone to help you. The fresh air will do her good. Make sure she keeps warm though."

Five minutes later Grandma, Leah and I were out on the terrace at a spot where there was a view through the railings. Lined up below us were parked cars and I could see someone trying to maneuver a red Volvo into a narrow space in the middle of the row. As views went it left a lot to be desired but I had chosen the spot in the hope it might trigger Grandma's memory of the lawns and the river that had once been there because I was sure she must have played at Riverside House when she was a little girl. I gave her time to orientate herself and then I asked her.

It took her so long to answer that I thought she was having one of those bad days when nothing seemed to fix itself in her head. She wasn't though and when she finally spoke her voice sounded younger, as if she was back in her childhood.

"We used to fish for minnows," she said. "There was a river then, and grass, and we used to fish for minnows.

The excitement I'd felt earlier returned. "Who else was with you?" I asked.

"Aunt Sarah and Harry and Grace. Aunt Celia as well, and the new baby. Uncle Robert used to come too when he was feeling strong enough."

"Why was Uncle Robert poorly?"

She shrugged as she replied in her little girl voice. "He wasn't poorly he just didn't like noise. It was because of the guns he heard when he was a soldier. We always had to be quiet when he was with us."

"And did you mind being quiet?"

"Harry did, but I didn't, and nor did Grace, because we always caught more minnows when Uncle Robert came with us. He knew where to find them you see. Nobody else did." Her voice held all the contempt of a small child.

I was searching for another question when she spoke again and this time there were bubbles of laughter in her voice as she lifted her shaky old hand and pointed. "Look, he's wearing his silly hat again, the one with the feathers in it."

I looked and saw him too. He was tall and very thin, and although his hair was hidden beneath a cloth hat that was sporting an assortment of fishing flies, I could tell it was very dark. His eyes were bright blue and luminous with laughter as he listened to the chattering of the small children skipping and running beside him. As Grandma and I watched, they all made their way down to the river and that was when Ma and Rebecca arrived.

The sound of their voices jolted us back to the present. I didn't care though because I had seen Robert, and apart from the thinness and the hollows beneath his cheeks, which were probably the result of his wartime experiences, he looked exactly as I had imagined he would. He was the image of his father, that dashing young man in the photo, the one who had turned the heads of all the village girls at a cricket match so long ago. He had the same upright figure and, despite his laughter, the same determined mouth. He also looked so much like my Robbie Parker that I determined to destroy the one photo we had of him as soon as I possibly could.

I wondered if Arthur had ever suspected he wasn't his own flesh and blood but even if he had, I knew without any doubt that he would have pushed the thought away and refused to allow it to destroy the life he had with Rose. For a moment I despised him for his weakness, then I realized it was love not weakness that would have kept him silent. I turned to Ma and my sister. They had their backs to me as they bent to kiss Grandma. She looked at me over Ma's shoulder, and although I can still hardly believe it, I swear she winked at me.

Chapter Seventeen

The next couple of days were uneventful apart from the fact that I couldn't get enough of Daniel and, although I didn't deserve it, he couldn't get enough of me. I'm not going to share what went on between us once Leah was asleep though, because there are limits. Besides, a lot of other things were about to happen and when I was at home on my own I spent most of my time preparing for them.

For a start, Ella was back in touch. Instead of texting me, she had called early one morning while I was clearing up the stewed apple and yoghurt Leah had managed to smear across her highchair. My shriek of delight probably blasted her eardrum but she didn't complain, and by the time we finished talking she had agreed to come to Mapleby to see her Dad. I could tell she felt guilty for leaving it so long, the same as I could tell there was something going on in her life that she didn't want to talk about. I had a feeling the two were intertwined but I didn't ask. I didn't mention Robbie either because I wasn't sure what her reaction would be, so to keep things fair I didn't tell him she was coming either.

Ella sorted, I now had to talk to Millie. It took a lot of courage to walk into the shop and face her again, and I certainly didn't deserve the warm greeting she gave me. For a moment I was speechless, then I turned to Daniel.

"Is it okay if Millie and I go upstairs for a coffee?"

"Be my guests," he said. "I'll call for help in the unlikely event that we get inundated with customers."

Millie laughed and I poked my tongue out. It was two o'clock in the afternoon, too early for the school run and way past the time people dropped by for a sandwich or something from the deli. It was the middle of the week too, so not the day most people did their grocery shopping.

Hefting Leah onto my hip, I followed Millie up the wooden stairs at the back of the storeroom. They were covered with splashes of white paint. "Is Robbie going to sand these down?" I asked her.

She looked at the paint as if she had never noticed it before. "I don't know. I haven't asked him."

Her tone of voice told me everything I needed to know and I could have kicked myself. Of course she hadn't noticed a few blobs of paint on the stairs, she was too intent on getting a roof over her head, somewhere dry and safe for her children. I had a sudden picture of Leah and me with nowhere to go and no close family to turn to and felt ashamed I had ever given her a hard time.

"It's not important," I said. "I'll ask him about it when I next see him."

"Thank you. You see him most days don't you, now he's renovating the house next to yours."

Wondering if that piece of information had come from Robbie or Daniel, or someone else entirely, and not liking the fact that our daily coffee break seemed to be common knowledge, I just nodded. Then I asked her if I could look around the apartment. She stared at me in surprise.

"It's yours, Rachel, you don't have to ask to look at it."

"Yes I do, because it's going to be your home so for all I know you've already started putting up curtains and things."

I was trying to be nice, to make up for all the mean thoughts I'd had about her, I wasn't trying to make her cry. I did though. Great gulping sobs that smeared her mascara and made her nose run. I dug into my bag for a tissue and came up with some of Leah's baby wipes. When she saw them, Millie gave a shaky laugh.

"They'll do a much better job than a tissue," she said, taking one and wiping all her make-up away.

Seeing her with a shiny nose and freckles did wonders for my confidence even though I was long past wondering if Daniel was tempted by her. She saw the expression on my face and managed another smile. "It's all camouflage. Underneath I'm a total mess."

169

Deciding the tour of the apartment could wait, I led her into the kitchen and made her sit down. Then I plopped Leah onto her lap while I made the coffee. Unlike the last time they'd met, Leah was full of smiles. She also found Millie's long red ponytail a source of fascination and proceeded to pull it hard.

"Ouch! That hurts, sweetie," Millie distracted her by bouncing her up and down while she sang a nursery rhyme. I watched them while I waited for the kettle to boil and saw that she genuinely liked children. She was a more natural mother than me, someone who would always cope in an emergency. Leah would not only be safe; she would enjoy the extra attention.

I finished making the coffee and put it on the table in front of her, just out of Leah's reach. "Do you want me to take over now?" I asked.

"Not unless you want to. It's a long time since I cuddled such a little one. I love that special baby smell they have." She suddenly looked wistful. "Much as I love my boys, I always wanted a little girl."

"Well now you can have one for three hours, five days a week," I said.

"Are you really sure about it, Rachel? It sounded a good idea when Daniel told me he thought you were bored staying at home all the time, but afterwards, when I had time to think about it, I wondered if it was how you really felt, or if Daniel was misreading things. Believe me, men do that sometimes," she added bitterly.

Her concern was enough for me to forget how angry I'd been when I learned that she and Daniel had been discussing me behind my back. It was enough, too, for me to suggest to her the idea that had been niggling away at the back of my mind ever since Leah had pulled her hair.

"I'm quite sure," I said firmly. "Besides she'll only be upstairs when I'm working in the shop so you can always call me if she needs me. And there's something else I'd like you to consider too. What about us doing alternate Saturdays as well? We can share the children between us."

She stared at me. "Would you really do that; have the boys I mean?"

"Well, I'd have to get to know them first so maybe we should try half a day at the beginning, but yes I'm happy to give it a try. Daniel says they are very nice little boys, well behaved and polite."

She smiled then. "I've threatened them to ever be anything else but good when they are in the shop. They're okay though, which is a miracle given everything they've been through in their short lives."

I didn't want to pry so I just agreed, but she seemed determined to get everything out in the open. "In case you're wondering, they never see their father. He lives in Spain now, with a girl who is almost young enough to be his daughter. I wish her the best of luck with him if she ever decides she wants children."

She saw the question in my eyes even though I tried to hide it, and her mouth twisted into a painful smile. "He was fine until Liam was born but once the excitement of being a new dad was over, the responsibility began to pall. Because I'd read all the books I knew fathers could sometimes be jealous in the early days, so I gave him as much attention as I could and waited for him to get over it. He didn't though, and then we fell for Connor. I didn't intend to have another baby so soon, but because I love children it didn't really bother me. It bothered him though, so much so that he hit me."

She stopped then, one hand over her mouth while the other clutched Leah. "I've never told anyone that before. I'm sorry. I'll understand if you don't want me to look after Leah now you know I couldn't even keep my own family safe."

I stopped her. "Please, Millie don't say another thing. If we start swapping confidences there are plenty of things I could tell you that I'm ashamed of, and maybe I will one day. In the meantime, you still have to show me around your new home."

By the time we rejoined Daniel, Millie and I were close to being friends. We walked to the school together when it was time for her to collect her little boys, and when they came running out and saw Leah in her pram they begged to be allowed to push her. I expected them to argue when Millie said no, but they didn't. Instead they walked either side of me and talked to Leah. Impressed, I asked them about their day and learned it was bug week.

"They mean National Insect Week," Millie told me, laughing at my confusion. "Almost every lesson has a bug connection. They've been writing about them, drawing them, counting their legs, and putting them in glass jars so they can examine them. "

"'Cept my teacher makes us set them all free at the end of every day," Connor told me indignantly.

I smiled at him. "I don't think they'd enjoy living in school all the time, do you?"

He looked doubtful. "I don't think they'd mind spending a week there, or I could bring them home and they could live with me."

His brother, barely a year older, shook his head scathingly. "You know we're not allowed to have pets where we live, and we won't be able to have them when we move, either. You can't keep bugs in a shop, they might get in the food."

In for a penny, in for a pound. "You can come and look at the bugs in my garden anytime you like," I said.

"Really and truly?" Connor's face lit up with excitement.

Thinking of all the greenfly, ants and ladybirds that populated my garden, to say nothing of the beetles, centipedes and spiders, I nodded. "How about you come on Saturday while your Mummy is moving into your new home?"

* * *

Of course I forgot the Trayners were arriving on Saturday when I made my impetuous offer, the same as I forgot about Ella. It was only when Robbie arrived the following morning and helped me finish the last of the choc chip cookies that I remembered. I groaned.

"What's the problem?" he asked, wiping crumbs from his mouth with the back of his hand. Even though I was right back on Daniel, I couldn't help noticing that he had a beautiful mouth, sculpted but firm, and set above a cleft chin that made his otherwise very handsome face slightly quirky. For a moment I was ashamed of my thoughts but then I realized that looking is very different from wanting, and I went back to enjoying the view even as I explained what I'd done.

"They'll be looking forward to a quiet visit while they make final decisions on the décor for the house, and instead the next door garden will be full of small boys collecting bugs and shouting at the top of their voices."

He laughed out loud at that. "You do love to exaggerate, don't you? Two small boys aren't exactly overkill and besides all you have to do is tell them the bugs will hide from them if they make too much noise and your non-existent problem is solved."

"Do you always have an answer for everything?"

"If only," he gave me a dark look before finishing his coffee in a single gulp and going back to his building. As I watched him walk down the path I remembered Ella and wondered if I would ever learn to think before I spoke.

* * *

Saturday dawned bright and clear, like most days that summer. I was up and dressed by six o'clock much to Daniel's amusement. "Anyone who didn't know better would think it was you who was moving, not Millie."

173

I handed him a mug of coffee. "At least you're getting coffee in bed and that doesn't happen very often, so be grateful."

He grinned at me, well it was more of a leer actually. "I can think of something I'd much rather have."

"In your dreams, mister. This is Millie's day so I'm going to make a cake to welcome her to her new home, and a casserole too, so she doesn't need to cook this evening. You can give her sandwiches from the shop at lunchtime."

"Yes, Ma'am," he sketched a salute. "Are there any more orders, Ma'am?"

I threw a balled up sock at him. "Yes. You can get Leah when she wakes up."

* * *

Rose was waiting for me in the kitchen, which sort of surprised me. Now I knew all her secrets I expected her to leave me alone. "I'm not going to tell anyone about you," I said, as I reached for the mixing bowl.

She smiled but she didn't go. She just sat there, on one of the kitchen chairs, and watched me as I beat butter and sugar together, added the eggs and flour, and spooned the mixture into a cake tin. At first I was irritated but then I calmed down, and by the time I put the cake in the cooker I felt positively mellow.

I glanced at Rose and she smiled again. Had she turned up to keep me calm, or had she come to see the Trayners? Then the truth hit me as clearly as if I'd heard her speak. She was here for Robbie. He might not be her own flesh and blood but he was linked to her precious son through his great-great-grandfather, the original Robert Parker, so she wasn't going until she had sorted out his life as well as mine.

I shook my head. "You're a witch, not a ghost, Rose Davis. I just hope you are as successful with Robbie as you were with me, then perhaps we can all have a bit of peace."

174

"Are you practicing your welcome speech for the Trayners?" Daniel teased as he came through to the kitchen with Leah.

I banged a few pans about so I could pretend I hadn't heard him but he knew I had and I heard him chuckling as he carried Leah out into the garden to greet the morning.

"You certainly know how to complicate my life," I told Rose, turning back to where she was sitting, but of course she had gone.

When Daniel came back indoors, leaving wet footprints all over the floor because of the dew on the grass, I was chopping vegetables while meat and spices browned in a pan on the hob. He sniffed appreciatively. "I hope you're making two of those."

I gave him my best beady stare. "I'm making one large one and we are all going to eat it at Millie's."

His eyes widened in surprise. "Does she know?"

"She does. We arranged it yesterday. You can collect me and the children when the shop closes, and if Ella has arrived by then, she can come too."

"Well put the flags out, Ella's coming to Mapleby. Come on, Rachel, you don't really believe that do you, not after she's let everyone down so many times? Besides, Tom hasn't said a thing and he would tell anyone who would listen if she really was coming."

"He hasn't said a thing because he doesn't know," I told him. "I talked to her on the phone and told her how he's not coping so well these days and that's when she said she'd come."

"But you daren't tell him in case she bails out again," he said, and then went into the bathroom whistling.

He was right of course, but I wasn't going to admit to it. I had to believe she was coming because if she let me down, I didn't have a back up plan for Robbie.

Chapter Eighteen

The next day I couldn't remember why I'd been so worried about everything because it all went as smooth as clockwork. Better in fact, but then I probably have Rose to thank for that.

With the cake finished and the casserole simmering, I took the car and collected Liam and Connor from Millie while Daniel and Leah ate their breakfast. The little boys were quiet on the way back to the cottage, probably because of the last thing Millie said to them as she strapped them into the car. "Be good," she whispered. "And be quiet, too, because Leah isn't used to noisy little boys."

Although I was pleased about the keeping quiet bit, I just smiled at her. "Don't worry Millie, they'll be fine. We will all be fine. You just go and turn those rooms into a home."

She straightened up and hugged me. "I'll never be able to repay you and Daniel. Never!"

"What nonsense," I told her as brusquely as I could because I didn't want tears again, from either of us. I was glad about the hug though.

Daniel and Leah were waiting for us at the gate. Robbie was there too, looking smarter than usual in new jeans and an open necked shirt instead of his working gear. They both smiled at me and then turned to greet the little boys as they burst excitedly from the car.

"Wow, this is an ENORMOUS garden," Liam peered over the gate in awe.

"It really isn't," I said but he stopped listening the moment Daniel swung open the gate to let him through. His brother followed without a word, and in less than a minute the pair of them had disappeared behind the house. I started after them, conscious that they were my responsibility for the rest of the day, but Daniel grabbed my arm.

"They'll be fine," he said. "This is the only way out of the garden and the fence is secure, so you don't have to keep them under surveillance all day."

"But what if one of them falls over and hurts himself, or a bee stings them or...or..." I knew there were several other catastrophes waiting to happen, I just couldn't think of one right then.

Both men laughed at me. "They're searching for bugs," Robbie said. "Not trekking down the Amazon."

I scowled at them. "It's not funny. What do I know about boys and bugs? This is a really, really bad idea."

"No it's not, it's a very good idea, and a kind one too," Daniel handed me Leah and gave us both a swift kiss on the cheek. "I must go or I'll be late opening up. I'll be back for all four of you later, and for Ella too if she keeps her promise."

I didn't look at Robbie until the car was just a puff of exhaust in the distance. When I finally plucked up courage he was waiting. "When were you going to tell me?" he said.

I shook my head. "I wasn't. I just hoped that when you saw each other again everything would fall into place."

"Like a fairytale, you mean. I'm afraid life's not like that Rachel. What went wrong between Ella and me will need a lot more than a cleverly contrived meeting to put it right."

"If that's the case, then why did you come to Mapleby without telling her?" I asked him. "Was it because you hoped she'd run into your arms when she saw you again, all your quarrels forgotten?"

He had the grace to look sheepish. I shook my head in mock despair but then I took pity on him and explained my plan.

"If she comes at all, she'll go to see Tom first and then she'll come to the cottage to see me, except I might not be here if she's late. I might be eating a casserole with Millie and the boys to celebrate them moving into their new home. You can come too if you like because you did most of the work, that's if you are too much of a coward to stay here on your own and wait for Ella."

Given that I was making it up as I went along, it wasn't a bad challenge. He didn't buy it though. "I can't do that, Rachel. She will never forgive me, or you, if we force her into a corner."

I was still thinking how best to answer him when a big black range rover stopped on the verge beside us and the driver wound down the window. "Is that Orchard House?" he asked, pointing next door. When Robbie said it was, he stuck his hand through the window. "Jerry Trayner," he said.

Just at that moment Liam and Connor reappeared around the side of the house and came careering down the path to where I was standing at the gate. "Rachel, Rachel, come and see what we've found," they yelled at the very top of their voices. "It's an ant nest and when we poked it with a stick all the ants got mad and ran about the grass."

"One bit me," said Connor, "but I squished it."

I closed my eyes very briefly. When I opened them again the children had multiplied. Now there were four small boys hopping up and down on the path, all wanting to look at the ants and have a turn with the stirring stick. Jerry Trayner laughed.

"Apologies," he said in an attractive American drawl. "They've been cooped up in airplanes and hotels since Wednesday, so energy levels are a bit high. Sam and Bailey, come and introduce yourselves."

The boys, who were a little older than Liam and Connor, but not much, stopped leaping around and came over to where I was standing. The oldest one held out his hand. "Hi. My name is Samuel Trayner and I'm very pleased to meet you, Ma'am."

We shook on it and I marveled as much at his beautiful manners and his cute accent as I did at how such a small hand could produce such a firm handshake. Then I turned to his brother. "That means you must be Bailey Trayner. Well, I'm Rachel Ryan and I live here, right next door to your new house, so if you'd like to come and play with Connor and Liam, you are very welcome."

"That's so kind but we mustn't let them bother you," a small, blonde woman had climbed down from the car while I'd been talking and now she was standing beside me looking flustered.

I smiled at her. "The matter has been taken out of both our hands, so let's just enjoy the peace while it lasts."

She returned my smile as she watched her sons disappear around the back of the cottage. All four children were chattering nineteen to the dozen, as if they'd known one another for years. "You can say that again. Travelling to England and then spending two nights in London followed by a long car journey has just about finished all of us. If I have to listen to the buzz of another electronic game this side of Christmas, I swear I'll go mad."

"Well, that settles it. You go and look at your new house, and when you've finished you can come and have coffee and cake while you regroup."

She grasped my hand. "That sounds great Rachel. I'm Marcie by the way. And who is this little angel?" She brushed her fingers across Leah's plump legs.

"This is Leah and we both like your new house," I told her.

"Well hello, Leah. How come your Mom can cope with you as well your brothers, when I get worn out with two?"

I laughed. "The boys aren't mine. I'm just minding them for their mother."

"Well thank goodness. For a moment I thought I was moving next door to wonder woman, what with coffee and cake being on offer as well."

"Hurry up, Marcie." Jerry Trayner had engaged Robbie in serious conversation while I was talking to his wife, but now he was getting impatient. Marcie rolled her eyes as she went to join him, a mutinous act which left me grinning as I watched them pick their way through the building equipment and go into the house.

* * *

By the time they arrived for coffee I had spread raspberry jam between the two layers of the sponge cake I had originally made for Millie, and sprinkled the top with sugar. Marcie clapped her hands when she saw it.

"Look Jerry, a real English Victoria sponge cake. No frosting or cream, just preserves and sugar. Please say you make scones and cucumber sandwiches, too?"

I laughed that anyone could think I was some sort of culinary expert. "No I don't, and there's nothing special about the cake. I just make it the way my mother showed me"

"And I guess her mother showed her." She plumped herself down in a chair, her eyes shining with enthusiasm.

"You'll have to forgive Marcie," Jerry apologized as he joined her at the table. "She writes cookbooks."

I pushed the cake towards Marcie. "In that case you had better cut it. I don't want to expose my crooked slicing technique to an expert."

She laughed and obliged while I poured coffee and offered cream and sugar, and then Robbie called the boys who, after a cursory washing of hands, sat outside on the grass eating cake and drinking squash.

We talked about the cottage while we drank our coffee, or rather the Trayners talked and Robbie and I listened, me enviously as they explained what else they wanted doing, and Robbie seriously because it was his job. Once they finished discussing hot tubs and walk-in wardrobes and a whole lot of other things beside, and when we had finished the last crumb between us, Marcie started talking about the cake again.

"It was great," she said. "Is it a family recipe?"

I nodded. "It's probably been in the family for generations because I can even remember my grandmother making it and she probably learned from her own mother."

"Nothing written down though?"

I started to shake my head, then I remembered something I had skimmed past in one of Rose's diaries. It had been a recipe for a special cake she had decided to make for her

180

mother's birthday. "I might be able to find something," I said slowly. "I'll let you know when I next see you."

That was when I suddenly remembered everything I knew about the Trayners. Until then I had been so beguiled by Marcie and the little boys that it had gone clean out of my head. Now I turned to Jerry Trayner and said what I should have said when I first met him.

"Actually I think you and I might be distantly related."

He stared at me doubtfully. "Ryan you said, Rachel Ryan. No, it's not a name on our family tree."

"That's because she's married, dummy," his wife told him. Then she turned to me. "What was your name before it was Ryan, honey?"

"Pavelak," I said. "But it's not that one either. My Great-Great-Aunt May was Sarah Trayner's mother."

"You're kidding," Jerry actually went a bit pale. "I wasn't expecting a cousin half a dozen times removed to be my new next door neighbor."

I was a bit taken aback as well because although I knew there had to be some sort of family link, I hadn't expected it to be that direct. Once we had recovered from our mutual surprise he told me Sarah Trayner was his great-grandmother and that after she and her husband died, their youngest son moved to America.

"He was my grandfather and when he married he settled in a small town in Oregon and abandoned his English roots. Now we're going to be living in England, I'm trying to find them again. I know there are a whole bunch of Trayners in London," he said. "And a few more in the English midlands, but to find someone who still lives where it all started, well, that's really something."

I laughed then, loving his enthusiasm and the way both he and Marcie were so friendly and relaxed. "You might regret saying that because there are a whole lot of us in Mapleby."

By the time I'd finished explaining the numbers and complications of the Pavelak clan, it was lunchtime.

"Let's all go eat," Jerry said, putting his head outside the kitchen door and whistling for the boys.

They came at a run, Liam and Connor happy to follow the older boys' lead. Leah was awake too, and cheerful after her mid morning nap. I protested of course, but he insisted, dismissing my worries about taking too many children into the local pub with the unconcern of a parent who knows his children will behave at the table. I didn't have the same sort of confidence about Millie's boys because I didn't know them well enough, and I knew Leah would deliberately dribble her food out of her mouth if she didn't like it, but I decided to go with the flow anyway, and soon we were all strapped into the range rover while Robbie followed on behind in his van.

I had thought he might refuse at first but when our eyes met he gave a little nod and I knew he was telling me that if Ella was at the pub and they bumped into one another, then he would deal with it. I gave him my most sympathetic smile. Then I went to change Leah's nappy while he helped Jerry load the children into the car.

* * *

Ella was the first person we saw, of course. She was standing behind the bar helping Tom serve a sudden influx of lunchtime customers. They both looked up when the door opened and for a moment we were at the receiving end of a pair of professional welcoming smiles, then Tom's widened into the sort of grin that said all his Christmases had come at once. He shouted to be heard above the clatter of knives and forks and the buzzy conversation of his customers.

"Look who the wind has blown in Rachel."

I smiled and waved as I shepherded my portion of our party towards an empty table. Ella started to wave back but her arm froze in midair, as did her smile. Behind me Robbie muttered something under his breath and I knew his courage had deserted him and he was about to bail out.

182

"Oh, no, you don't," I said, grabbing his arm. Then, in my brightest voice I proceeded to organize the table, ushering him in between Liam and Connor so there was no chance of escape. He glowered at me but I just gave him a sweet smile before I turned to Marcie.

"I need the biggest favor. That girl behind the bar is one of my oldest friends and I haven't seen her in months because she lives and works away. Would you mind very much if I abandon you for five minutes while you find out what the children want to eat? I just need to say hello and show her Leah because she hasn't seen her since she was tiny."

"You go ahead, honey. Just say what you want and I'll do the rest."

"Oh…um…I'll have a lemonade and um…fish and chips." It was the only thing I could remember that was always on the menu.

I left her discussing food with the children and an almost silent Robbie and hurried across to the bar. Ella was waiting for me and her greeting was anything but friendly.

"What are you up to?" she said, her voice tight with anger. Tom was busy with a customer so she didn't have to worry about upsetting him.

"Me up to something? I have no idea what you're talking about," I feigned innocence with very little hope of success because Ella and I had known one another for far too long for her to be taken in. I was right.

"Robbie Parker," she hissed. "Did he put you up to this because you can go and tell him from me, right now, that it's not going to work. Oh and by the way, there's nothing wrong with my Dad so the next time you bring me down here get your facts right first."

If she hadn't said that I might not have lost my temper, but her apparent disregard for Tom's health did it for me, and she knew she had gone a step too far when I answered. "So you think he's fine, do you? Well, that makes your life very easy doesn't it? You can carry on gadding about the world and mixing with your millionaire celebrities because your Dad's okay. I expect he's already told you he doesn't want you to feel responsible for him anyway, hasn't he?" It was a guess but I could see it hit home.

"Well maybe it hasn't occurred to you in the five minutes you've been here that he's good at hiding things. If you watch him instead of thinking about yourself all the time, you'll notice how he struggles to pick up the bottles and glasses and how, when he thinks nobody is looking, he massages his fingers and thumbs. And maybe you haven't noticed it yet, but there's a stool behind the bar which never used to be there, and if you watch him you'll find he uses it whenever he can to take the weight off his feet."

I peered over the bar, in full flow now although I kept my voice low. "And those shoes he's wearing, he's put them on in your honor today, which means his feet will hurt like hell when he's in bed tonight. Usually he wears slippers, you see. Smart ones, slippers that look like shoes at a quick glance, but they don't kid any of the customers who have known him since he was Mapleby's brightest star, the man the whole village gathered to watch whenever he played rugby."

I could see I'd shocked her and it should have given me some satisfaction. It didn't, though, because I knew I should have made her visit Mapleby sooner, before Tom was almost overtaken by misery. The trouble was I had been too wrapped up in myself and my own problems. Ridiculous as they were, they hadn't left any room for other people, even Daniel, and I felt ashamed all over again.

Before I could say another word, however, Tom joined us, his smile so wide it threatened to split his face in half. Fortunately, Jerry arrived with the order at the same time, and by the time he had placed it, and I had made introductions all round, it was time for me to return to our table.

"We'll catch up later," I told Ella, giving her a smile that was full of meaning.

She nodded for the benefit of her father and Jerry but even though I knew I'd shocked her I also knew she wasn't about to forgive my subterfuge about Robbie. When we did find the time to talk I was going to be in a whole lot of trouble.

When I returned to the table I gave Leah to Marcie while I went to find a highchair, and by the time I found one, our drinks had arrived. With Leah securely strapped in and far too interested in what was going on around her to cause any immediate trouble, I sank into my own chair with a sigh and took a long drink from my glass of lemonade.

"Good huh?" Jerry said, taking a sip from his own glass.

I nodded and then, at his request, filled him in on the history of Riverside House since his family sold it to the council. When I added the fact that my ninety-four-year-old grandmother was living there he was more than excited.

"We must go visit. Do you hear that Marcie, Rachel's grandmother is still alive at ninety-four and living in the old family home?"

Robbie and I shook our heads in unison. "It was pulled down years ago to make room for a modern nursing home," we told him. "There's nothing left for you to see."

"Except your grandmother," Marcie said. "Would she mind if we visited her?"

"I know she'd love to see you if she's having a good day. Unfortunately she suffers from vascular dementia so her memory is unreliable, and sometimes she just sleeps through an entire visit."

"I guess we'll risk that," Jerry said. Then he gave me a puzzled look. "If the old house was pulled down years ago and most of the garden turned into a parking lot, how come you know so much about how it looked? Are there photos, because your description of the lawns sloping down to the river, and the huge stone planters full of flowers make it sound as if you've actually seen it?"

Robbie saved me. "Rachel found her great-great-grandmother's diaries from way back and she's been reading them in an attempt to piece together her family history."

"Which is why you knew we were distant cousins," Jerry's eyes were shining with excitement. "May I look at those diaries, Rachel? They sound like great material for a book."

Marcie interrupted him with a burst of laughter. "I said you wouldn't last a morning without letting it slip."

She turned to me. "Jerry writes historical novels in his spare time. He's pretty successful although he pretends to be modest about it. You might have heard of him. He writes as R. J. Archibald."

Jerry gave a self-deprecating laugh. "Always choose a name at the front of the alphabet. It gets noticed first."

I stared at him. "I can't believe it. R. J. Archibald is one of my mother's favourite writers."

"Not yours. though?" He grinned at me.

"Not yet but there's always time," I said, and laughed even while I wondered how I could keep him away from Rose's diaries. What with Marcie wanting me to find the recipe I'd seen in one of the notebooks, Robbie's mother asking to see them, and Jerry wanting to read all of them, it was going to be difficult to keep Rose's secret unless I did something drastic, like burning them.

While I was still worrying about it the meals arrived and took my concentration for the next few minutes as children demanded ketchup and I searched for a rusk to keep Leah busy while we ate. After that the conversation turned to the more mundane but Robbie didn't relax and nor did I. Although he said all the right things and smiled in the right places, his eyes keep flicking towards the bar. He didn't smile at me either and I knew that was because I'd trapped him in between Millie's two little boys. Unable to slide out of the bench he was sitting on without disrupting the whole table, he could neither escape nor confront Ella. I gave an inward sigh. Before the day was over I was going to be in a lot of trouble with two very angry people, and I still had to decide what to do about Rose's diaries.

Chapter Nineteen

Of course I was reckoning without Rose's help, so when I glanced towards the bar to see if Ella was still there, I nearly choked on my food because Rose was sitting in a chair beside the fireplace. In cold weather Tom made sure there was always a crackling fire burning but now the weather was warmer there was just a display of flowers set right in the middle of the empty hearth.

Marcie handed me a glass of water. "Are you okay, honey?"

"I'm fine," I lied. "A piece of fish went down the wrong way."

It was at that point that Tom came over to check we were all enjoying the food. We assured him we were and then Jerry asked him a few questions about the history of the pub. Tom's answer nearly had me choking again.

"More than half of it is an extension," he said, waving his arm towards the other end of the pub and the room beyond. "It was added years ago before I bought the place, but I've seen the plans and whoever did it was very careful to preserve an authentic look."

Jerry nodded. "What with the name and all those old tools and dainty Victorian shoes on display, I'm guessing the original part of the building was a cobbler's workshop."

Tom nodded. "Yes, not that I can tell you anything about it except that all this stuff was found in a cupboard by the person in charge of the renovations. He made a note about it on the plans, but if he did find out anything about who used to live here, he kept it to himself."

"Well, that's a shame," Jerry turned to me. "Add it to your research Rachel. It might turn out to be another member of our family."

I knew he was joking so I managed a smile. Behind me I could sense Rose shaking her head. She didn't need to

187

worry though because I had no intention of telling them anything, ever.

"There's one other thing," said Tom, turning back to the table when he was almost at the point of walking away. "See the small wooden chest where we store the menus. It contained a set of old fashioned baby clothes, an ivory rattle, and that tiny pair of shoes you can see hanging above the mantle when I found it. It was wedged under a shelf at the back of the cellar which must be why the builder missed it."

We all turned to stare at the tiny shoes. They were blue and the ribbon that attached them to a nail driven into the wall was blue, too. They were about the size a child would wear when it took its first steps. I wanted to touch them and something in my expression must have conveyed that to Tom because he walked across to the fireplace and lifted them down while Rose watched him.

I took them in my hands and as my fingers cupped the soft leather I had the swiftest flash of a little boy's face laughing up at me. He had Robbie's blue eyes and he wasn't much older than Leah. As the vision faded I turned to look at Rose but the chair was empty.

While the others exclaimed over the shoes and asked Tom about the other items in the box, I wondered why I had never noticed that the pub was full of old memorabilia, most of it shoe related. Also, the clue was in the name. The Cobbler's Arms. I felt really stupid until I remembered that everything I had learned about Rose and Arthur was new to me. Until very recently I hadn't known anything about them at all and it was this that allowed me to ask Tom a final question.

"Do you think they lived here, the cobbler and his family, or was it just his place of work?"

Tom smiled as he answered. "They almost certainly lived here. According to the plans this room was probably the family sitting room, and the storage area behind the bar was the kitchen and scullery before it was knocked into one. The actual cobbler's shop was at the front of the house with a door directly onto the street."

Jerry nodded, wearing what was almost certainly his serious historian's face. "There would have been a wooden counter too and the room was probably small and dark and not very comfortable. The poor man would have spent his days perched on a high stool making shoes for the whole village."

I maintained an expression of intelligent fascination with the whole subject while all the while telling myself that it was why Rose had looked so relaxed sitting by the empty hearth. This had been her home, the place where her children were born, and right now I was sitting in the room where I had last seen her and Arthur. I looked around but there was nothing I remembered, nothing to connect it to Rose except for the baby shoes that Marcie had just passed to Robbie.

As he took them his eyes widened and I guessed that just for a moment he had caught a glimpse of his history. Then Leah began to cry, and by the time I had soothed her and begun to spoon pureed vegetables into her ever open mouth, the shoes were hanging above the mantle again.

* * *

"Coffee?" Jerry wasn't ready to leave yet, which meant Robbie and I had to stay as well, Robbie because he was working for him, and me because I was without transport. Counting heads, he went over to the bar and placed the order. When he came back, he was smiling.

"The landlord says he'll bring our coffee outside so we can sit in the sunshine and the children can go back to their bug hunting."

The four little boys didn't need a second invitation. They were out of the door before he finished talking. I called after them, reminding Liam and Connor not to go near the road or the car park.

Robbie, released at last from the middle of the bench, said he'd go and keep and eye on them while I repacked Leah's bag and took her to the bathroom to change her nappy yet again. Marcie came with me so she could reapply her lipstick and brush her hair, and by the time we joined the others in the garden we felt as if we were old friends. I knew I was going to love having her as my next door neighbor.

She laughed as we approached the table. "We seem to be collecting people."

She was right. A couple of the regulars, vey old men who could remember what the building had been like before the extension was added, were talking to Jerry. He waved an apology. "Don't mind me, I'm just getting another history fix."

Marcie shook her head in mock disgust. "He does this all the time. I'm going to ignore him while you tell me all about Mapleby." I started to say something but when I saw who was sitting with Robbie, my tongue stuck to the roof of my mouth.

"Hello. I hope you don't mind me joining you but your husband insisted," Ella told Marcie.

"Of course not. You're the friend Rachel hasn't seen in ages, aren't you, so how about I push this gorgeous baby over to the pond where we will look at the ducks while you catch up on your news."

We all protested and said she should at least drink her coffee first, but she just shrugged. "I'm not really into coffee. Give it to Jerry when he starts calling for a second cup." Then she turned to me. "You don't mind do you, Rachel? I won't go any further, I promise."

I shook my head, only too glad she wouldn't be around to see what was coming to me, and when Liam and Connor asked me if they could go as well, I said yes with more enthusiasm than was strictly necessary. I watched them set off in silence, noting how, although the road was completely devoid of traffic, Marcie made all the children stop and look both ways before releasing them to rush across the grass to the pond on the village green.

"You're going to have to look at us eventually, Rachel," I was so surprised by the hint of laughter in Robbie's voice that I spilled my coffee.

"I'll fetch a cloth," Ella jumped up, ever the landlord's daughter. Robbie caught her hand.

"Promise you'll come back."

She nodded as she gently disengaged herself. He watched her walk across the garden and then he turned back to me. "We've a lot of talking to do but I think it's going to be okay, thanks to you."

I stared at him in total disbelief. "What happened while Marcie and I were in the bathroom, and I won't take anything less than a miracle as an explanation?"

He gave a wry smile. "Ella brought out the coffee. I don't think she realized it was for us. Anyway, when he saw her Jerry remembered she was an old friend of yours so he insisted she join us, and before she could say no, he had ordered another cup of coffee from one of the waitresses."

"So she had to sit down?"

"Yes, although if she had sat any closer to the edge of her seat she'd have fallen off."

"And she talked to you?"

"Actually, no. She listened, and then she pretended she had something in her eye so I wouldn't know she was crying."

"You did though?"

"Yes, and when I asked her why, she said it was too complicated to explain, so I said 'try me' and that's where we were when you came back with Marcie."

So you don't know yet?"

He shook his head. "No, but I intend to find out if it takes me all day."

"Would you like me to go so you can talk in private?"

He shook his head again. "I don't think so. Whatever the problem is, it affects all of us, Tom, you, me, her other friends in the village, so you have every right to want answers as well."

I saw Ella coming towards us with a cloth in her hand, and frowned. "She might not like being outnumbered."

"Actually it will be a relief," I hadn't meant for Ella to hear what I said but she waved my apology away.

"If I don't tell you both now, I'll never tell anyone," she said, blotting up the spilt coffee with more concentration than it warranted.

We waited, and eventually she folded up the cloth and squared it to the corner of the table. Then she fiddled with her rings. Eventually Robbie took hold of her hands and forced her to look at him. "Sitting here thinking about it is only making it worse. Talk to us Ella?"

At first she was hesitant, picking and choosing her words and talking in a monotone, but once we started asking questions she relaxed just enough for me to recognize the old Ella, and my heart bled for her.

* * *

"So let me get this right, when you first met this guy, this so called celebrity, he was all over you, so much so that you had an affair. It was only later you found out he had taken a video of you having sex?" Robbie's fury wasn't directed at Ella but at the man she was telling us about.

She nodded bitterly. "I was so young and naive, and I was in love...well that's what I told myself... so it never occurred to me he would do something like that, let alone blackmail me later. "

"And he's been threatening to put the pictures on the Internet for how long?"

"I don't know but it seems like forever," she lowered her head to hide her distress but we still saw the tears that plopped onto the table in front of her.

"So you do everything you can to keep him sweet because it's the only way you know to stop him carrying

192

out his threat?" Robbie tilted her chin to make her look at him.

"Not like that, not anymore, no. I just fly out to do his make up and hair when he asks me to," she shook her head, horrified that we might have the wrong idea.

Although I can't speak for Robbie, I'm ashamed to say the thought did cross my mind for just a second or two until I saw her face, then I knew she was telling the truth. Her brief affair with this dreadful man had been over long before she met Robbie. All that was left was a video of something so private that only a complete villain would use it to retain power over a girl he had once professed to love.

"It's okay," I told her, patting her arm. "We believe you. But what I don't understand is why. What does he expect to get out of it?"

Robbie's laugh was devoid of even a trace of amusement as he explained. "I don't know how good you are on celebrities, Rachel, but I've worked on enough film sets with Ella to know exactly who she's talking about. This man is a fading star. A very long time ago he could and probably did have any woman he wanted, but then he got older and his hair went gray, so when Ella fell for his charm, a girl whose make-up and hair dye kept him looking young, he took advantage. It was only afterwards he remembered she knew all about his gray hair and the Botox and the secret visits to his plastic surgeon, and he panicked until he found a way to keep her silent. He showed her the video and told her he would post it on the Internet if she ever breathed a single word about the work he's had done.

"Then, to make sure she took him seriously, he also told her what would happen if the Press got hold of it, and once she realized that photographers would turn up at The Cobbler's Arms hoping to get an up-to-date picture, and that they would talk to the customers about her, she stopped coming to Mapleby. You weren't prepared to put your father through that, were you?" He turned to Ella.

She shook her head miserably.

Swearing under his breath, he got up. "Look after her, Rachel. My guess is that Ella isn't the first girl he's done this to, but she's certainly going to be the last."

"No Robbie, please, you don't know what he might do to you," Ella grabbed at his hand but she was too late. In a moment he had gone, just stopping beside Jerry's table long enough to excuse himself, saying a sudden emergency had arisen.

Jerry nodded amiably and then returned to the elderly men who were still talking about the past, and for the first time in what seemed forever, Ella and I were alone.

"Why didn't you tell me?" I asked her.

"Because I didn't think you would understand." She found a tissue in her pocket and blew her nose.

I frowned, more than a little hurt. "Even if I didn't, I'd still have been there for you."

"I know you would, but it got so I couldn't bear to be with you and Daniel. Seeing the two of you so happy together just about killed me. It made me feel so ashamed too."

I sighed. "If only you knew. Daniel and I are fine now but I've been so mean to him ever since Leah was born that I'm surprised he's still with me."

She was silent for a long moment, then she slowly shook her head. "It's not the same, Rachel. Whatever you've done to Daniel, you still love him and he loves you, and I'll never believe otherwise whatever you tell me. I, on the other hand, allowed myself to be so dazzled by fame and money that I didn't see my ... him...for who he really is." She couldn't even bring herself to say his name.

"And you ran away from Robbie because you felt ashamed?"

"Yes, but I did it to protect him as well. What if I had married him and then, a few years later, that video had appeared on the Internet? I wasn't prepared to risk what it would do to him, what it would do to our relationship."

Chapter Twenty

Ella drove over to the cottage later that afternoon and made a fresh cake for Millie's party while I mashed potatoes and put the finishing touches to the casserole.

"All done," I said, as I packed the final dish into the large cardboard box Daniel had brought home from the shop the previous evening. Ella added the tin containing the cake and we gave one another a look of mutual satisfaction.

"You were so right," she told me. "Spending the afternoon with you and the children has taken me out of myself. I haven't had so much fun for ages."

Remembering the expression on her face when the little boys had insisted on showing her their bug farm, I grinned. "If you call this afternoon fun then you really do have a sad life."

Tears welled up in her eyes. "Don't joke about it, Rachel. I can't bear to think what's happening to Robbie right now, and anyway, even if he does manage to sort things out, he won't want to marry me, will he?"

"Why ever not? From where I was sitting at lunchtime, he's head over heels in love with you. Why else was he prepared to wait it out in Mapleby? Given his experience of building film sets, he could have been working anywhere in the world, instead of which he's been here for weeks just waiting and hoping you'll turn up."

"But that was before he knew. Now I've told him everything he won't want anything more to do with me."

I had far more faith in Robbie than that but I could see it wasn't worth arguing. Instead, searching around for something else to take her mind off her problems, I invited her to join us at Millie's.

"But won't she mind?" she asked. "It's not as if we've ever been friends."

"Believe me, she'll be pleased to see you, and she needs all the friends she can get." I gave her a potted version of Millie's life to date, including how she was going to look after Leah for me each afternoon so I could dip my toe back into the working world.

"She sounds so strong," Ella said and I heard the envy in her voice. I bit back the jokey remark I had been about to make and thought about it. She was right. Millie was strong, stronger than me and stronger than Ella. Was it just part of her character or had life forced it on her? There was no way of telling, but what I did know was that my last vestige of resentment had fallen away. I was glad Daniel had offered her a job, glad he had insisted about the rooms above the shop, glad that he had talked to her about me.

I nodded. "She is," I said.

* * *

The house party was a great success. As well as Ella, there was Daniel, Leah and me, Millie and her two boys, and her grandfather was there, too. He was very old and bent and he used two walking sticks, but he was sharp as a tack.

"You've done a good job here," he told Daniel, hobbling from room to room and poking at the walls with the end of one of his sticks. "I can rest easy now I know my granddaughter is somewhere safe."

Millie flushed slightly when she heard him. "I'm fine, Granddad. You never needed to worry about me."

He snorted. "I most certainly did, especially once that waste of space you called a husband left you, not that he was ever much use when he was here." He turned to me. "I can't understand why he wanted to leave anyone as beautiful as my Millie, can you? And to leave her with two little boys as well, it's beyond wicked."

I agreed with him and then, to save Millie from further embarrassment, changed the subject by asking him about himself. When he told me he lived in a nursing home I asked if it was the one in the village. He nodded. "So you know it, do you? Not where I wanted to end up really but I couldn't cope after my wife died. Gammy legs you see,"

I nodded understandingly. "My Grandma lives there, too."

He stared at me from under beetling brows. "Are you one of those Pavalak girls?"

"I was. I'm Rachel Ryan now."

"Yes, yes, I know that, but it's the past I'm talking about. There was a big house where the nursing home is now. It used to belong to your relatives. They weren't Pavalaks but they were connected to your family. I forget the name though."

"Trayner." I told him, and after that the conversation flowed as I regaled all that had happened that day including the lunch with Marcie and Jerry Trayner. Liam and Connor, not to be outdone, told everyone about their new American friends, and how they were going to play together every other Saturday when I looked after them.

"It doesn't sound like we're going to take it slowly after all," I said to Millie, laughing.

* * *

If only Ella had been happy it would have been a perfect evening. She tried. She smiled at everything and asked questions, and told stories about her work on different film locations around the world, and the celebrities she knew. She had brought some flowers for Millie too, and they added to the gaiety of the occasion, as did Leah who had just started to giggle and who found everything the little boys did hilarious. They played up to her of course, and in the end Millie had to call things to a halt when all three of them developed hiccups.

"I've had the best time," she told me as we washed up together in the kitchen afterwards. "And so has Granddad. He doesn't get out much and the boys get bored when we go to see him because his room is very small and they have to be quiet."

"Well, he'll be able to come and see you now, and maybe I can persuade him to visit my grandmother, after all they live in the same place."

"That would be nice. I know he misses having people to talk to who remember what Mapleby was like when he was young."

Recalling some of my conversations with Grandma, I grinned as I hung the wet tea towel over the sink. "I can't promise he'll get much sense out of her, but I'll introduce them when I next visit."

"When you do, ask him to tell her about Rose," she said.

I stared at her as goose bumps prickled along my arms. "Rose?"

"Yes. I don't know who she is but he often talks about her. At one time I thought she was someone who lived in one of the other rooms but when I asked, nobody had heard of her, so I think she must be a visitor. I expect she saw him sitting on his own and felt sorry for him. Hopefully I'll get to meet her one day."

I was just telling myself that I was getting het up about nothing when she spoke again. "It's a bit weird, actually. Mostly he just says he's seen her again, but one day a few weeks ago he asked me to get Daniel to visit him because he wanted to talk to him. I didn't have a clue what it was about and he wouldn't tell me. It was only afterwards, when Daniel said the boys and I could live over the shop, that I discovered Granddad had been put up to it by this Rose, whoever she is. Maybe she's one of your relatives, because although a lot of people know that you and Daniel own the shop, hardly anybody knew there was an apartment above it until I told them. Everyone just thought it was a storage space. You don't know anyone called Rose do you, Rachel?"

I shook my head, forcing a frown of puzzlement across my forehead. "Sorry I can't help. I don't know anyone in Mapleby who would do something like that."

It was almost the truth.

"What a day!" Daniel and I were lying in bed, arms and legs tangled, too sleepy to do anything but cuddle.

"Mmm," I nuzzled my face into his shoulder. "It was good though."

"Mostly thanks to you. If you hadn't offered to look after Liam and Connor and then produced enough food to feed an army, the whole day would have been much harder for Millie."

"Maybe," I snuggled closer. "But the best thing is having Ella back."

He moved his head and I felt his lips brush my hair. "Not as good as having the old Rachel back."

I slipped my hand under the sheet and began to stroke his chest. He tried to ignore it. "You said you'd tell me why she stayed away so long, and also why Robbie suddenly disappeared in a hurry. Am I right in guessing the two things are related?"

"You are but I don't want to talk about it now." My hand began to move south and that's when we discovered we weren't too sleepy after all.

Epilogue

Robbie never told anyone what happened. All I know is that he returned to Mapleby a couple of days later, handed Ella a DVD, and told her she could stop worrying. "It's the only copy and I would have destroyed it but I thought you might want to do that yourself."

"Have you...did you look at it?" she whispered, barely able to say the words.

"Of course I didn't and nor should you. Just get rid of it Ella. Jump on it, stamp on it, run the car over it, anything that'll help you forget what he did to you."

He didn't tell me himself, I heard it from Ella at the same time she told me she was going to stay in Mapleby for a while and help out at The Cobbler's Arms. "Dad wants to pay me a wage," she said, laughing. "Try as I might I can't convince him I've earned so much money in the past few years that I can afford to take a few month's break from work."

"Of course staying here for a bit has nothing to do with Robbie being in Mapleby," I teased her.

She grinned at me. Although she still had dark shadows under her eyes and was far too thin, she was beginning to look like the old Ella. "It might have."

"So he does still want to marry you."

"Yes, but I've told him we have to take it slowly. It's not that I don't love him, I just don't feel I'm good enough for him, Rachel. I feel sort of tarnished."

Remembering how hard Robbie flirted when the mood took him, I shook my head in disgust. "That's because his past is white as snow, is it? Don't tell me he hasn't done some stupid things of his own because we all have."

"I know he has but it doesn't make any difference. I can't move on until I'm ready and he says he's prepared to wait."

"Well be careful because he's a bit too dishy to leave lying around for someone else to pick up."

She laughed. "Don't worry. I'm not going to make him wait that long."

And that's when I knew it would be okay.

* * *

Leah was just two when she was flower girl at their wedding, and very cute she looked too in her little Victorian dress with its blue sash and a matching ribbon in her hair.

* * *

200

I loved being back in the shop and Leah loved spending time with Millie and the boys. I enjoyed my Saturdays with them too, especially once Marcie Trayner joined in and we began to take all the children on an outing from time to time. The days when we all piled into her big car and took off to spend a few hours at the seaside, or to visit a museum, or just took the children to kick a ball around on the village green were some of the best I remember from those times, and sometimes, when it was my turn to work, she would take Millie instead.

Whether Millie will ever risk another relationship I don't know and I don't ask her. I hope she does though, because she's a brilliant mother. She's a good friend too.

When I was pregnant the second time, she was marvelous, and so was Marcie. Between them they looked after Leah so often that Ma and my sisters started to complain they never saw her. I took no notice because it wasn't true. I still visited the farm, and Grandma, and my sisters, and it wasn't long before we all began to invite Millie and the boys as well as the Trayners to almost every family event.

What with all the usual Pavalak advice plus the more down to earth stuff from Millie and Marcie, and the constant messages from Ella whenever she and Robbie were away on location, plus working at the shop as well as looking after Leah and Millie's two little boys, I never had a moment to worry about my second pregnancy. I know Ma and my sisters were concerned when I first told them another baby was on the way, but Daniel just smiled and kissed me. He knew I was never going back into the shadowlands I had inhabited after Leah was born, and when the midwife handed him our little girl, he kissed her too.

"Hello Rose," he said.

* * *

I never did see my Rose again, not after the Trayners moved in next door. I looked for her from time to time because there was something important I wanted to tell her, but she never came back. She probably knows I burned her diaries anyway, all but the page with the Victoria sponge recipe printed in thick black ink. Marcie was so delighted I had found it that she devoted a whole chapter to it in her cookbook about traditional English cakes.

* * *

When Jerry asked if he could read the rest of the notebooks I pretended to be upset as I told him someone in the family had thrown them out by mistake. Well, it was only a little lie and I knew it was what Rose wanted. She would have hated her life plastered across the pages of an historical novel. Besides, I'd promised her I would keep her secret. So now all that's left is the horseshoe that Robbie fixed on my fence, and the tiny pair of blue shoes hanging above the mantle in The Cobbler's Arms, and they could have belonged to anyone.

The End

A special cake for Mama's birthday

I've never made a cake all on my own before but Mama said I could make this one as long as I followed her recipe exactly. It was such a success that I'm going to copy it into my diary so I never forget it. Making a Victoria sponge is much more exciting than mixing up a fruit cake or a plain old madeira cake because there's always a risk that it might not rise.

First I had to weigh out eight ounces of butter, then eight ounces of sugar, and then I had to beat them both together with a wooden spoon until they were white and fluffy.

After that I had to crack four eggs into a small bowl and stir them around with a fork until the yolk and the whites were all mixed in. It was a lovely color when I finished because the hens are laying well at the moment. It was a deep orangey yellow like the beginning of a sunset. Then came the tricky part. I had to pour the egg mixture into the fluffy butter and sugar just a little at a time and then beat it hard. Mama said if I tipped the whole lot in at once the mixture would curdle and spoil the cake.

When I was sure there wasn't even the tiniest bit of curdle, I measured out eight ounces of flour and added two teaspoons of baking powder to it. Then I gradually sifted the whole lot into the bowl through Mama's smallest sieve. All that was left to do after that was to mix everything together with a metal spoon. Mama showed me how to lift it up to get air into the mixture. If I had just stirred it round and round with the wooden spoon it would have probably come out flat. It didn't though. It came out of the oven like a puffed up golden moon, well two moons really because I had divided the mixture in half and put each half into a separate tin.

Greasing the tins with butter was the worst part, and then sprinkling flour over the butter and banging the tins on the side of the table to make sure it covered every little bit. I knew if I got that wrong it would be a disaster. The cakes would stick to the tin and I would have to patch up the broken bits the best I could. Fortunately it didn't happen, so I must have floured and greased them enough. The cakes slid onto the cooling rack beautifully, and once they were cold I put one on our very best plate, the green one with the pansies painted on it, and then I spread it with the preserve Mama made last summer when we had too many raspberries. I could have used the strawberry one if I had wanted to, but I like raspberry best. I licked the spoon clean when I finished.

Next I placed the other half of the cake on top of the jam and dusted the top with sugar. When I finished it looked magnificent. Papa said it was the best cake he had ever tasted and ate two slices!

May, who always seems to know everything, says it was invented by one the the Queen's ladies-in-waiting, the Duchess of Bedford I think she said. I suppose she called it the Victoria sponge to please her mistress. I was a bit fed up when May told us that because she always has to interrupt things, but then I didn't mind because she said it was good too, although she did add that when the Queen ate it she usually put a layer of cream over the jam as well. I told her this wasn't the Queen's cake, it was Mama's cake, and I said I am never ever going to put cream in it however many times I make it in the future.

Oh, I forgot to say. I cooked it in the oven at a medium temperature for about half-an-hour.

If you *loved* this book
(or even just liked it)

Please leave a review ...
Authors need reviews! Keep this author writing.

Other Books We Love titles by Sheila Claydon

Cabin Fever
Reluctant Date
Double Fault
Kissing Maggie Silver
Mending Jodie's Heart (Book 1: When Paths Meet)
Finding Bella Blue (Book 2: When Paths Meet)
Saving Katy Gray(Book 3: When Paths Meet)
Miss Locatelli

Sheila Claydon agrees with the late Ray Bradbury: *'First, find out what your hero wants. Then just follow him.'* She starts with plots, chapter outlines and characters; she knows all the rules and faithfully follows them each time she starts to write a new story. Then the hero takes over and she follows him instead.

She can be contacted on http://sheilaclaydon.com where her books are listed, and where she also writes an occasional blog. Also at facebook.com/SheilaClaydon.author and on twitter

www.ingramcontent.com/pod-product-compliance
Lightning Source LLC
Chambersburg PA
CBHW060049260626

47160CB00005B/1631